The Custodians

Richard Cowper

The Custodians

and other stories

Pan Books London and Sydney

Piper at the Gates of Dawn and *The Custodians*
first appeared in *Fantasy and Science Fiction Monthly*

This collection first published 1976 by Victor Gollancz Ltd
This edition published 1978 by Pan Books Ltd,
Cavaye Place, London SW10 9PG
© Colin Murry 1975 and 1976
ISBN 0 330 25364 6
Printed and bound in Great Britain by
Richard Clay (The Chaucer Press) Ltd, Bungay, Suffolk

Contents

for Judith and James Blish

The Custodians

Although the monastery of Hautaire has dominated the Ix valley for more than twelve hundred years, compared with the Jurassic limestone to which it clings it might have been erected yesterday. Even the megaliths which dot the surrounding hillside predate the Abbey by several millennia. But if, geologically speaking, Hautaire is still a newcomer, as a human monument it is already impressively ancient. For the first two centuries following its foundation it served the faithful as a pilgrims' sanctuary, then, less happily, as a staging post for the crusaders. By the thirteenth century it had already known both fat years and lean ones and it was during one of the latter that, on a cool September afternoon in the year 1272, a grey-bearded, sunburnt man came striding up the white road which wound beside the brawling Ix, and hammered on the Abbey doors with the butt of his staff.

There were rumours abroad that plague had broken out again in the southern ports and the eye which scrutinized the lone traveller through the grille was alert with apprehension. In response to a shouted request the man snorted, flung off his cloak, discarded his tattered leather jerkin, and raised his bare arms. Twisting his torso from side to side he displayed his arm-pits. There followed a whispered consultation within, then, with a rattle of chains and a protest of iron bolts, the oak wicket gate edged inwards grudgingly and the man stepped through.

The monk who had admitted him made haste to secure the door. 'We hear there is plague abroad, brother,' he muttered by way of explanation.

The man shrugged on his jerkin, looping up the leather toggles with deft fingers. 'The only plague in these parts is ignorance,' he observed sardonically.

'You have come far, brother?'

'Far enough,' grunted the traveller.

'From the south?'

The man slipped his arm through the strap of his satchel,

eased it up on to his shoulder and then picked up his staff. He watched as the heavy iron chain was hooked back on to its staple. 'From the east,' he said.

The door-keeper preceded his guest across the flagged court-yard and into a small room which was bare except for a heavy wooden trestle table. Lying upon it was a huge, leather-bound *registrum*, a stone ink pot and a quill pen. The monk frowned, licked his lips, picked up the quill and prodded it gingerly at the ink.

The man smiled faintly. 'By your leave, brother,' he murmured and taking the dipped quill he wrote in rapid, flowing script: '*Meister Sternwärts – Seher – ex-Cathay*'.

The monk peered down at the ledger, his lips moving silently as he spelt his way laboriously through the entry. By the time he was half-way through the second word a dark flush had crept up his neck and suffused his whole face. 'Mea culpa, Magister,' he muttered.

'So you've heard of Meister Sternwärts, have you, brother? And what have you heard, I wonder?'

In a rapid reflex action the simple monk sketched a flickering finger-cross in the air.

The man laughed. 'Come, holy fool!' he cried, whacking the door-keeper across the buttocks with his stick. 'Conduct me to Abbé Paulus lest I conjure you into a salamander!'

In the seven hundred years which had passed since Meister Sternwärts strode up the long white road and requested audience with the Abbé Paulus the scene from the southern windows of the monastery had changed surprisingly little. Over the seaward slopes of the distant hills, purple-ripe clouds were still lowering their showers of rain like filmy nets, and high above the Ix valley the brown and white eagles spiralled lazily upwards in an invisible funnel of warm air that had risen there like a fountain every sunny day since the hills were first folded millions of years before. Even the road which Sternwärts had trodden, though better surfaced, still followed much the same path, and if a few of the riverside fields had expanded and swallowed up their immediate neighbours the pattern of the stone walls was still recognizably what it had been for centuries. Only the file of high-tension cable carriers striding diagonally down across the valley on a stage of their march from the hydro-electric barrage in the high mountains thirty miles to the north proclaimed that this was the twentieth century.

Gazing down the valley from the library window of Hautaire, Spindrift saw the tiny distant figure trudging up the long slope; saw the sunlight glittering from blond hair as though from a fleck of gold dust; and found himself recalling the teams of men with their white helmets and their clattering machines who had come to erect those giant pylons. He remembered how the brothers had discussed the brash invasion of their privacy and had all agreed that things would never be the same again. Yet the fact remained that within a few short months they had grown accustomed to the novelty and now Spindrift was no longer sure that he could remember exactly what the valley had looked like before the coming of the pylons. Which was odd, he reflected, because he recalled very clearly the first time he had set eyes upon Hautaire and there had certainly been no pylons then.

May 1923, it had been. He had bicycled up from the coast with his scanty possessions stuffed into a pair of basket-work panniers slung from his carrier. For the previous six months he had been gathering scraps of material for a projected doctoral thesis on the life and works of the shadowy 'Meister Sternwärts' and had written to the Abbot of Hautaire on the remote off-chance that some record of a possible visit by the Meister might still survive in the monastery archives. He explained that he had some reason to believe that Sternwärts might have visited Hautaire but that his evidence for this was, admittedly, of the slenderest, being based as it was on a single cryptic reference in a letter dated 1274, sent by the Meister to a friend in Basle.

Spindrift's inquiry had eventually been answered by a certain Fr Roderigo who explained that, since he was custodian of the monastery library, the Abbé Ferrand had accordingly passed M. Spindrift's letter on to him. He was, he continued, profoundly intrigued by M. Spindrift's inquiry because in all the years he had been in charge of the Abbey library no one had ever expressed the remotest interest in Meister Sternwärts; in fact, to the best of his knowledge, he, Fr Roderigo, and the Abbé Ferrand were the only two men now alive who knew that the Meister had spent his last years as an honoured guest of the thirteenth-century Abbot and had, in all probability, worked in that very library in which his letter was now being written. He concluded with the warm assurance that any such information concerning the Meister as he himself had acquired over the years was at M. Spindrift's disposal.

Spindrift had hardly been able to believe his good fortune. Only the most fantastic chance had led to his turning up that letter in Basle in the first place – the lone survivor of a correspondence which had ended in the incinerators of the Inquisition. Now there seemed to be a real chance that the slender corpus of the Meister's surviving works might be expanded beyond the gnomic apophthegms of the *Illuminatum*! He had written back by return of post suggesting diffidently that he might perhaps be permitted to visit the monastery in person and give himself the inestimable pleasure of conversing with Fr Roderigo. An invitation had come winging back, urging him to spend as long as he wished as a lay guest of the Order.

If, in those far-off days, you had asked Marcus Spindrift what he believed in, the one concept he would certainly never have offered you would have been predestination. He had survived the war to emerge as a Junior Lieutenant in the Supply Corps and, on demobilization, had lost no time in returning to his first love, Medieval Philosophy. The mindless carnage which he had witnessed from the sidelines had done much to reinforce his interest in the works of the early Christian Mystics with particular reference to the *bons hommes* of the Albigensian Heresy. His stumbling across an ancient handwritten transcript of Sternwärt's *Illuminatum* in the shell-shattered ruins of a presbytery in Armentières in April 1918 had, for Spindrift, all the impact of a genuine spiritual revelation. Some tantalizing quality in the Meister's thought had called out to him across the gulf of the centuries and there and then he had determined that if he were fortunate enough to emerge intact from the holocaust he would make it his life's work to give form and substance to the shadowy presence which he sensed lurking behind the *Illuminatum* like the smile on the lips of the Gioconda.

Nevertheless, prior to his receiving Fr Roderigo's letter, Spindrift would have been the first to admit that his quest for some irrefutable evidence that the Meister had ever really existed had reaped but one tiny grain of putative 'fact' amid untold bushels of frustration. Apparently, not only had no one ever *heard* of Sternwärts, they expressed not the slightest interest in whether he had ever existed at all. Indeed, as door after door closed in his face, Spindrift found himself coming to the depressing conclusion that the Weimar Republic had more than a little in common with the Dark Ages.

Yet, paradoxically, as one faint lead after another petered out or dissolved in the misty backwaters of Medieval hearsay, Spindrift had found himself becoming more and more convinced, not only that Sternwärts *had* existed, but that he himself had, in some mysterious fashion, been selected to prove it. The night before he set out on the last lap of his journey to Hautaire he had lain awake in his ex-army sleeping sack and had found himself reviewing in his mind the odd chain of coincidences that had brought him to that particular place at that particular time: the initial stumbling upon the *Illuminatum*; the discovery of the cryptic reference coupling Sternwärts with Johannes of Basle; and, most fantastic of all, his happening to alight in Basle upon that one vital letter to Johannes which had been included as a cover-stiffener to a bound-up collection of addresses by the arch-heretic Michael Serventus. At every critical point it was as though he had received the precise nudge which alone could put him back on the trail again. 'Old Meister,' he murmured aloud, 'am I seeking *you*, or are you seeking *me*?' High overhead a plummeting meteor scratched a diamond line down the star-frosted window of the sky. Spindrift smiled wryly and settled down to sleep.

At noon precisely the next day he pedalled wearily round the bend in the lower road and was rewarded with his first glimpse of the distant Abbey. With a thankful sigh he dismounted, leant, panting, over his handlebars and peered up the valley. What he saw was destined to remain just as sharp and clear in his mind's eye until the day he died.

Starkly shadowed by the midday sun, its once-red tiled roofs long since bleached to a pale biscuit and rippling in the heat haze, Hautaire, despite its formidable mass, seemed oddly insubstantial. Behind it, tier upon tier, the mountains rose up faint and blue into the cloudless northern sky. As he gazed up at the Abbey, Spindrift conceived the peculiar notion that the structure was simply tethered to the rocks like some strange airship built of stone. It was twisted oddly askew and some of the buttresses supporting the Romanesque cupola seemed to have been stuck on almost as afterthoughts. He blinked his eyes and the quirk of vision passed. The massive pile re-emerged as solid and unified as any edifice which has successfully stood four-square on the elements for over a thousand years. Fumbling a handkerchief from his pocket, Spindrift mopped the sweat from his forehead, then, remounting his bicycle, he pushed off on the last lap of his journey.

Fifteen minutes later, as he wheeled his machine up the final steep incline, a little birdlike monk clad in a faded brown habit fluttered out from the shadows of the portico and scurried with arms outstretched in welcome to the perspiring cyclist. 'Welcome, Señor Spindrift!' he cried. 'I have been expecting you this half hour past.'

Spindrift was still somewhat dizzy from his hot and dusty ride but he was perfectly well aware that he had not specified any particular day for his arrival if only because he had no means of knowing how long the journey from Switzerland would take him. He smiled and shook the proffered hand. 'Brother Roderigo?'

'Of course, of course,' chuckled the little monk and, glancing down at Spindrift's bicycle, he observed: 'So they managed to repair your wheel.'

Spindrift blinked. 'Why yes,' he said. 'But how on earth ...?'

'Ah, but you must be so hot and tired, Señor! Come into Hautaire where it is cool.' Seizing hold of Spindrift's machine he trundled it briskly across the courtyard, through an archway, down a stone-flagged passage, and propped it finally against a cloister wall.

Spindrift, following a pace or two behind, gazed about him curiously. In the past six months he had visited many ecclesiastical establishments but none which had given him the overwhelming sense of timeless serenity that he recognized here. In the centre of the cloister yard clear water was bubbling up into a shallow limestone saucer. As it brimmed over, thin wavering streams tinkled musically into the deep basin beneath. Spindrift walked slowly forward into the fierce sunlight and stared down into the rippled reflection of his dusty, sweat-streaked face. A moment later his image was joined by that of the smiling Fr Roderigo. 'That water comes down from a spring in the hillside,' the little monk informed him. 'It flows through the very same stone pipes which the Romans first laid. It has never been known to run dry.'

A metal cup was standing on the shadowed inner rim of the

basin. The monk picked it up, dipped it, and handed it to Spindrift. Spindrift smiled his thanks, raised the vessel to his lips and drank. It seemed to him that he had never tasted anything so delicious in his life. He drained the cup and handed it back, aware as he did so that his companion was nodding his head as though in affirmation. Spindrift smiled quizzically. 'Yes', sighed Fr Roderigo, 'you have come. Just as he said you would.'

The sense of acute disorientation which Spindrift had experienced since setting foot in Hautaire persisted throughout the whole of the first week of his stay. For this Fr Roderigo was chiefly responsible. In some manner not easy to define the little monk had succeeded in inducing in his guest the growing conviction that his quest for the elusive Meister Sternwärts had reached its ordained end; that what Spindrift was seeking was hidden here at Hautaire, buried somewhere among the musty manuscripts and incunabula that filled the oak shelves and stone recesses of the Abbey library.

True to his promise the librarian had laid before Spindrift such documentary evidence as he himself had amassed over the years, commencing with that faded entry in the thirteenth-century *registrum*. Together they had peered down at the ghostly script. 'Out of Cathay,' mused Spindrift. 'Could it have been a joke?'

Fr Roderigo pulled a face. 'Perhaps,' he said. 'But the hand is indisputably the Meister's. Of course he may simply have wished to mystify the brothers.'

'Do you believe that?'

'No,' said the monk. 'I am sure that what is written there is the truth. Meister Sternwärts had just returned from a pilgrimage in the steps of Apollonius of Tyana. He lived and studied in the East for ten years.' He scuttled across to a distant shelf, lifted down a bound folio volume, blew the dust from it, coughed himself breathless, and then laid the book before Spindrift. 'The evidence is all there,' he panted, smiling shyly. 'I bound the sheets together myself some thirty years ago. I remember thinking at the time that it would make a fascinating commentary to Philostratus' *Life of Apollonius*.'

Spindrift opened the book and translated the brief and firmly penned Prolegomenon. '*Being then in my forty-ninth year, Sound in Mind and Hale in Body, I, Peter Sternwärts, Seeker after*

13

*Ancient Truths; Alerted by my Friends; Pursued by mine Enemies;
did set forth from Würzburg for Old Buda. What here follows is the
Truthful History of all that Befell me and of my Strange Sojourn in
Far Cathay, written by my own hand in the Abbey of Hautaire in
this year of Our Lord 1273.'*

Spindrift looked up from the page and, as he did so, he gave a
deep sigh of happiness.

Fr Roderigo nodded. 'I know, my friend,' he said. 'You do
not have to tell me. I shall leave you alone with him.'

But Spindrift was already turning the first page.

That evening, at Fr Roderigo's suggestion, Spindrift strolled
with him up on to the hillside above Hautaire. The ascent was a
slow one because every fifty paces or so Fr Roderigo was con-
strained to pause a while to regain his breath. It was then that
Spindrift became aware that the friendly little monk was ill.
Beneath that quick and ready smile were etched the deep lines of
old familiar pain. He suggested gently that perhaps they might
just sit where they were but Fr Roderigo would not hear of it.
'No, no, my dear Spindrift,' he insisted breathlessly. 'There is
something I must show you. Something that has a profound
bearing upon our joint quest.'

After some twenty minutes they had reached one of the fallen
menhirs that formed a sort of gigantic necklace around the
Abbey. There Fr Roderigo paused and patted his heaving
chest apologetically. 'Tell me, Señor,' he panted. 'What is
your candid opinion of Apollonius of Tyana?'

Spindrift spread his hands in a gesture that contrived to be
both non-committal and expiatory. 'To tell the truth I can
hardly be said to have an opinion at all,' he confessed. 'Of course
I know that Philostratus made some extraordinary claims on his
behalf.'

'Apollonius made only one claim for *himself*,' said Fr
Roderigo. 'But that one was not inconsiderable. He claimed to
have foreknowledge of the future.'

'Yes?' said Spindrift guardedly.

'The extraordinary accuracy of his predictions led to his
falling foul of the Emperor Nero. Apollonius, having already
foreseen this, prudently retired to Ephesus before the monster
was able to move against him.'

Spindrift smiled. 'Precognition obviously proved a most
useful accomplishment.'

'Yes and no,' said Fr Roderigo, ignoring the irony. 'Have you reached the passage in the Meister's *Biographia* where he speaks of the *Praemonitiones*?'

'Do they really exist?'

The little monk seemed on the point of saying something and then appeared to change his mind. 'Look,' he said, gesturing around him with a wide sweep of his arm. 'You see now how Hautaire occupies the exact centre of the circle?'

'Why, so it does,' observed Spindrift.

'Not fortuitous, I think.'

'No?'

'Nor did he,' said Fr Roderigo with a smile. 'The Meister spent a whole year plotting the radiants. Somewhere there is a map which he drew.'

'Why should he do that?'

'He was seeking to locate an Apollonian nexus.'

'?'

'The concept is meaningless unless one is prepared to accept the possibility of precognition.'

'Ah,' said Spindrift guardedly. 'And did he find what he was looking for?'

'Yes,' said Fr Roderigo simply. 'There.' He pointed down at the Abbey.

'And then what?' inquired Spindrift curiously.

Fr Roderigo chewed his lower lip and frowned. 'He persuaded Abbé Paulus to build him an observatory – an "*oculus*" he called it.'

'And what did he hope to observe from it?'

'*In* it,' corrected Fr Roderigo with a faint smile. 'It had no windows.'

'You amaze me,' said Spindrift, shaking his head. 'Does it still exist?'

'It does.'

'I should very much like to see it. Would that be possible?'

'It might,' the monk admitted. 'We would have to obtain the Abbot's permission. However, I—' He broke off, racked by a savage fit of coughing that turned his face grey. Spindrift, much alarmed, patted his companion gently on the back and felt utterly helpless. Eventually the little monk recovered his breath and with a trembling hand wiped a trail of spittle from his blue lips. Spindrift was horrified to see a trace of blood on the white handkerchief. 'Hadn't we better be making our way back?' he suggested solicitously.

Fr Roderigo nodded submissively and allowed Spindrift to take him by the arm and help him down the track. When they were about half-way down he was overcome by another fit of coughing which left him pale and gasping. Spindrift, now thoroughly alarmed, was all for going to fetch help from the Abbey, but the monk would not hear of it. When he had recovered sufficiently to continue he whispered hoarsely: 'I promise I will speak to the Abbot about the *oculus*.'

Spindrift protested that there was no hurry but Fr Roderigo shook his head stubbornly. 'Fortunately there *is* still just time, my friend. Just time enough.'

Three days later Fr Roderigo was dead. After attending the evening Requiem Mass for his friend, Spindrift made his way up to the library and sat there alone for a long time. The day was fast fading and the mistral was beginning to blow along the Ix valley. Spindrift could hear it sighing round the buttresses and mourning among the crannies in the crumbling stonework. He thought of Roderigo now lying out on the hillside in his shallow anonymous grave. *The goal ye seek lies within yourself.* He wondered what had inspired the Abbot to choose that particular line from the *Illuminatum* for his requiem text and suspected that he was the only person present who had recognized its origin.

There was a deferential knock at the library door and a young novice came in carrying a small, metal-bound casket. He set it down on the table before Spindrift, took a key from his pocket and laid it beside the box. 'The Father Superior instructed me to bring these to you, sir,' he said. 'They were in Brother Roderigo's cell.' He bowed his head slightly, turned, and went out, closing the door softly behind him.

Spindrift picked up the key and examined it curiously. It was quite unlike any other he had ever seen; wrought somewhat in the shape of a florid, double-ended question mark. He had no idea how old it was or even what it was made of. It looked like some alloy – pewter, maybe? – but there was no discernible patina of age. He laid it down again and drew the casket towards him. This was about a foot long, nine inches or so wide and perhaps six inches deep. The oak lid, which was ornately decorated with silver inlay and brass studding, was slightly domed. Spindrift raised the box and shook it gently. He could hear something shifting around inside, bumping softly against the sides. He did not doubt that the strange key unlocked the casket but when he came to try he could find no keyhole in which to fit it. He peered underneath. By the trickle of waning light through the western windows he could just discern an incised pentagram and the Roman numerals for 1274.

His pulse quickening perceptibly, he hurried across to the far end of the room and fetched an iron candlestick. Having lit the candle he set it down beside the box and adjusted it so that its light was shining directly upon the lid. It was then that he noticed that part of the inlaid decoration appeared to correspond to what he had previously assumed to be the handle of the key. He pressed down on the silver inlay with his fingertips and thought he felt it yield ever so slightly.

He retrieved the key, adjusted it so that its pattern completely covered that of the inlay, and then pressed downwards experimentally. There was a faint *click*! and he felt the lid pushing itself upwards against the pressure of his fingers. He let out his pent breath in a faint sigh, detached the key, and eased the lid back on its hinge. Lying within the box was a vellum-covered book and a quill pen.

Spindrift wiped his fingers along his sleeve and, with his heart racing, dipped his hand into the casket and lifted out the book. As the light from the candle slanted across the cover he was able to make out the faded sepia lettering spelling out the word: *PRAEMONITIONES* and below it, in a darker ink, the cynical query – *Quis Custodiet Ipsos Custodes?*

Spindrift blinked up into the candlelight. 'Who will watch the watchers?' he murmured. 'Who, indeed?'

The wind snuffled and whimpered against the now dark window panes and the vesper bell began to toll in the Abbey tower. Spindrift gave a violent, involuntary shiver and turned back the cover of the book.

Someone, perhaps even Peter Sternwärts himself, had stitched on to the fly leaf a sheet of folded parchment. Spindrift carefully unfolded it and peered down upon what, at first glance, seemed to be an incomprehensible spider's web of finely drawn lines. He had been staring at it for fully a minute before it dawned on him that the dominant pattern was remarkably similar to that on the lid of the casket and its weirdly shaped key. But there was something else too; something that teased at his recollection; something he knew he had once seen somewhere else. And suddenly he had it: an interlinked, megalithic spiral pattern carved into a rockface near Tintagel in Cornwall; here were exactly those same whorled and coupled 'S' shapes that had once seemed to his youthful imagination like a giant's thumbprints in the granite.

No sooner was the memory isolated than he had associated this graphic labyrinth with the pagan menhirs dotting the hillside round Hautaire. Could *this* be the map Roderigo had mentioned? He held the parchment closer to the quaking candleflame and at once perceived the ring of tiny circles which formed a periphery around the central vortex. From each of these circles faint lines had been scratched across the swirling whirlpool to meet at its centre.

Spindrift was now convinced that what he was holding in his hands was some arcane chart of Hautaire itself and its immediate environs, but at the precise point where the Abbey itself should have been indicated, something had been written in minute letters. Unfortunately the point happened to coincide with the central cruciform fold in the parchment. Spindrift screwed up his eyes and thought he could just make out the words '*tempus*' and '*pons*' – or, possibly, '*fons*' – together with a word which might equally well have been '*cave*' or '*carpe*'. 'Time', 'bridge', or perhaps 'source'. And what else? 'Beware'? 'Seize'? He shook his head in frustration and gave it up as a bad job. Having carefully refolded the chart, he turned over the fly-leaf and began to read.

By the time he had reached the last page the candle had sunk to a guttering stub and Spindrift was acutely conscious of an agonizing headache. He lowered his face into his cupped hands and waited for the throbbing behind his eyeballs to subside. He had, to the best of his knowledge, been intoxicated only once in his life and that was on the occasion of his twenty-first birthday. He had not enjoyed the experience. The recollection of how the world had seemed to rock on its foundations had remained one of his most distressing memories. Now he was reminded of it all over again as his mind lurched drunkenly from one frail clutching point to the next. Of course it was a hoax; an extraordinarily elaborate, purposeless hoax. It *had* to be! And yet he feared it was nothing of the sort; that what he had just read was, in truth, nothing less than a Medieval prophetic text of such incredible accuracy that it made absolute nonsense of every rationalist philosophy ever conceived by man. Having once read the *Praemonitiones* one stepped like Alice through the looking glass into a world where only the impossible was possible. But *how*? In God's name *how*?

Spindrift removed his hands from before his eyes, opened the book at random, and by the vestige of light left in the flapping candle flame, read once more how, in the year 1492, Christobal Colon, a Genoese navigator, would bow to the dictates of the sage Chang Heng and would set sail into the west on the day of the Expulsion of the Jews from Spain. He would return the following year, laden with treasure and 'companioned by those whom he would call Indians but who would in truth be no such people.' At which point the candle flared up briefly and went out.

Next morning Spindrift requested, and was granted, an audience with the Abbot. He took with him the wooden casket and the mysterious key. His eyes were red-rimmed and bloodshot and the dark rings beneath them testified to a sleepless night.

Abbé Ferrand was in his early fifties – a stalwart man with shrewd eyes, ash grey hair and bushy eyebrows. His upright stance struck Spindrift as having more than a touch of the military about it. He wore the simple brown habit of his Order, and only the plain brass crucifix, slung on a beaded leather thong about his neck, distinguished him from the other monks. He smiled as Spindrift entered the study, then rose from behind his desk and held out his hand. Spindrift, momentarily confused, tucked the casket under his left arm and then shook the proffered hand.

'And how can I be of service to you, M'sieu Spindrift?'

Spindrift took a breath, gripped the casket in both hands and held it out in front of him. 'Abbé Ferrand, I . . .' he began, and then dried up.

The corners of the Abbot's lips were haunted by the ghost of a smile. 'Yes?' he prompted gently.

'Sir,' blurted Spindrift, 'do you know what's in here?'

'Yes,' said the Abbot. 'I think I do.'

'Then why did you send it to me?'

19

'Brother Roderigo wished me to. It was one of his last requests.'

'The book's a forgery, of course. But you must know that.'

'You think so, M'sieu?'

'Well, of course I do. What else could it be?'

'And what makes you so certain?'

'Why,' cried Spindrift, 'because it *has* to be!'

'But there have always been prophets, M'sieu Spindrift,' returned the Abbot mildly. 'And they have all prophesied.'

Spindrift waved a dismissive hand. 'Nostradamus you mean? Vague ambiguities. Predictions of disaster which could be interpreted to fit any untoward circumstance. But this . . .'

The Abbot nodded. 'Forgive me asking, M'sieu,' he said, 'but what was it exactly that brought you to Hautaire?'

Spindrift set the casket down on the desk in front of him and laid the key beside it. As he did so he realized, not for the first time, that the question Abbé Ferrand was posing could have no simple answer. 'Principally, I believe, Peter Sternwärts' *Illuminatum*,' he said. 'I felt a compulsion to learn all I could about its author.'

The Abbot appeared to ponder on this reply, then he turned on his sandalled heel, walked over to a wall cupboard, opened it and drew from within another vellum-covered notebook similar in appearance to that which Spindrift had replaced in the casket. Having closed the cupboard door the Abbot stood for a moment tapping the notebook against his finger ends. Finally he turned back to Spindrift. 'I take it you have studied the *Praemonitiones*, M'sieu Spindrift?'

Spindrift nodded.

'Then you will perhaps recall that its forecasts end with the Franco–Prussian war. Unless my memory deceives me, the final entry concerns Bazaine's surrender at Metz in October 1870; the capitulation of Paris in 1871; and the signing of the treaty at Frankfurt-sur-Main on May 10th of that same year?'

'Yes,' said Spindrift, 'that is perfectly correct.'

The Abbot opened the book he was holding, flipped over a few pages, glanced at what was written there and then said: 'Would you say, M'sieu Spindrift, that Europe has at last seen the end of war?'

'Why, certainly,' said Spindrift. 'The League of Nations has outlawed—'

'On September 1st, 1939,' cut in the Abbot, 'Russia and Germany will, in concert, invade Poland. As a direct consequence of this Britain and France will declare war on Germany.'

'But that's preposterous!' exclaimed Spindrift. 'Why, the Versailles Treaty specifically states that under no circumstances is Germany ever again to be allowed to rearm!'

The Abbot turned back a page. 'In 1924 – next year, is it not? – Lenin will die and will be succeeded by' (here he tilted the page to catch the light) 'Joseph Viss-ar-ionovitch – I think that's right – Stalin. An age of unparalleled tyranny will commence in the so-called Soviet Republic which will continue for fifty-one years.' He flicked on. 'In 1941 German armies will invade Russia and inflict massive defeats on the Soviet forces.' He turned another page. 'In July 1945 the fabric of civilization will be rent asunder by an explosion in an American desert.' He shrugged and closed up the book, almost with relief.

'You are surely not asking me to believe that those fantastic predictions are the work of Peter Sternwärts?' Spindrift protested.

'Only indirectly,' said the Abbot. 'Without Meister Sternwärts they would certainly never have come into existence. Nevertheless he did not write them himself.'

'Then who did?'

'These last? Brother Roderigo.'

Spindrift just gaped.

The Abbot laid the book down on the desk beside the casket and picked up the key. 'Before he died,' he said, 'Brother Roderigo informed me that you had expressed a desire to examine the *oculus*. Is this so?'

'Then it really does exist?'

'Oh yes. Most certainly it exists. This is the key to it.'

'In that case I would very much like to see it.'

'Very well, M'sieu,' said the Abbot, 'I will conduct you there myself. But first I should be intrigued to know what makes you so certain that the *Praemonitiones* is a forgery?'

Spindrift looked down at the casket. The whorled inlay on its lid seemed to spin like a silver catherine wheel. He dragged his gaze away with difficulty. 'Because I have always believed in free-will,' he said flatly. 'To believe in the *Praemonitiones* would be to deny it.'

'Oh,' said the Abbot, 'is that all? I thought perhaps you had detected the alteration in the script which takes place at roughly fifty year intervals. It is admittedly slight but it cannot be denied.'

'The light was not good in the library last night,' said Spindrift. 'I noticed no marked change in the cursive style of the entries.'

The Abbot smiled. 'Look again, M'sieu Spindrift,' he said. 'By daylight.' He pressed the key into the lock, removed the *Praemonitiones* from the casket and handed it over.

Spindrift leafed through the pages, then paused, turned back a few, nodded, and went on. 'Why yes,' he said. 'Here in this entry for 1527. "The Holy City sacked by the armies of the Emperor Charles". There *is* a difference. How do you account for it?'

'They were written by different hands,' said the Abbot. 'Though all, I hazard, with that same pen.'

Spindrift reached into the casket, took out the cut-down quill and examined it. As his fingers closed round the yellowed shaft it seemed to twist ever so slightly between them as though endowed with some strange will of its own. He dropped it back hastily into the box and flushed with annoyance at his own childishness. 'If I understand you, Abbé, you are saying that these predictions were made by many different hands over the past seven centuries.'

'That is correct. It would appear that the horizon of foresight is generally limited to about fifty years, though in certain cases – notably Sternwärts himself – it reaches a good deal further.' The Abbot said this in a quiet matter-of-fact tone that Spindrift found distinctly disconcerting. He reached out tentatively for the second book which the Abbot had placed on the desk but, seemingly unaware of Spindrift's intention, the Abbot had casually laid his own hand upon it. 'Now, if you are ready, M'sieu,' he said, 'I suggest we might climb up and pay our respects to the *oculus*.'

Spindrift nodded.

The Abbot smiled and seemed pleased. He placed the two books within the casket and clapped the lid shut. Then he picked up the key, took down another bunch of keys which was hanging from a hook on the wall, and, nodding to Spindrift to follow him, led the way along a cool white corridor, up a flight of stone stairs and along a passage buttressed by slanting sunbeams.

They took several turns and climbed yet another flight of stairs. Spindrift glanced out of a window as they passed and observed that they were now almost on a level with the ruin of the pre-historic stone circle. The Abbot's leather sandals slapped briskly against the soles of his bare feet and made a noise like a razor being stropped.

At last they reached a small oak door. The Abbot paused, selected one of the keys from the bunch, thrust it into the lock and twisted it. The hinges groaned and the door squealed inwards. 'This leads to the dome of the rotunda,' he explained. 'The *oculus* is actually situated within the fabric of the northern wall. It is certainly an architectural curiosity.'

Spindrift ducked his head, passed through the doorway, and found himself in a narrow crack of a curved passage-way dimly lit by narrow barred slits in the outer stone-work. Thick dust lay on the stone floor which was caked with a crust formed from generations of bird and bat droppings. The floor spiralled up-wards at an angle of some ten degrees and Spindrift calculated that they had made at least one complete circuit of the rotunda before the Abbot said: '*Ecce oculus!*'

Peering past the broad shoulder of his guide Spindrift saw a second door, so narrow that a man could have passed through it only with extreme difficulty. The Abbot squeezed himself back-wards into a niche and allowed Spindrift to edge round him. Then he handed over the key to the casket, saying as he did so: 'You will find that it operates in the normal way, M'sieu.'

'Thank you,' said Spindrift, taking the key from him and approaching the door. 'Is there room for only one person inside?'

'Barely that,' said the Abbot. 'The door opens outwards.'

Spindrift inserted the key into the lock and twisted it. The wards grated reluctantly but still allowed the key to turn. Then, using it as a handle, for there was, indeed, no other, he pulled the door gently towards him. A moment later he had started back with a barely suppressed gasp of astonishment. The door had opened to disclose a sort of lidless limestone coffin, bare and empty, standing on its end, apparently cemented fast into the surrounding masonry. 'What on earth is it?' he demanded.

The Abbot chuckled. 'That is your *oculus*, M'sieu.'

Spindrift eyed the coffin uncertainly. 'And you say Stern-wärts built that?' he inquired dubiously.

23

'Well, certainly he must have caused it to be built,' said the Abbot. 'Of that there can be little doubt. See there—' He pointed to some lettering carved on the limestone corbel which framed the 'head' of the casque – *Sternwärts hoc fecit.* 'Not proof positive, I grant you, but good enough for me.' He smiled again. 'Well, now you are here, M'sieu Spindrift, are you not tempted to try it?'

Spindrift gazed at the Latin lettering. 'Sternwärts made this,' he muttered and, even as he spoke the words aloud, he knew he would have to step inside that stone shell, if only because to refuse to do so would be to deny the noble and courageous spirit of the man who had penned the *Illuminatum.* Yet he could not disguise his reluctance. How dearly at that moment he would have liked to say: 'Tomorrow, perhaps, or next week, if it's all the same to you, Abbé.' But he knew he would be allowed no second chance. It was now or never. He nodded, drew a deep breath, swallowed once, stepped resolutely forward and edged himself backwards into the cold sarcophagus.

Gently the Abbot closed the door upon him and sketched over it a slow and thoughtful sign of the Cross.

For no particular reason that he was aware of Spindrift had recently found himself thinking about Fr Roderigo. Once or twice he had even wandered out into the Abbey graveyard and tried to locate the spot where the bones of the little monk were buried. He had pottered about, peering vaguely among the hummocks, but he found that he could no longer recall precisely where the body of his friend had been interred. Only the abbots of Hautaire were accorded headstones and even Abbé Ferrand's was by now thickly encrusted with lichen.

Spindrift found a piece of dry twig and began scratching at the lettered limestone, but by the time he had scraped clean the figures '1910–1937' he found the impulse had already waned. After all, what was the point? That was the surprising thing about growing old: nothing seemed quite so urgent or important any more. Sharp edges became blunt; black and white fudged off into comfortable grey; and your attention kept wandering off after stupid little tit-bits of memory and getting lost among the flowery hedgerows of the Past. *Quis Custodiet . . . ?*

The old librarian straightened up, released the piece of twig he was holding, and began massaging his aching back. As he did so he suddenly recalled the letter. He had been carrying it around with him all day and had, in fact, come out into the graveyard on purpose to try to make up his mind about it. Obscurely he felt he needed the ghostly presence of Roderigo and the Abbé Ferrand to help him. Above all he needed to be *sure*.

He peered around for a convenient seat then lowered himself creakily so that his back rested against the Abbé's sun-warmed headstone. He dipped around inside his woollen habit for his spectacles and the envelope and having at last settled everything to his comfort and satisfaction he extracted the letter, unfolded it, cleared his throat and read out aloud:

> Poste Restante
> Arles
> Bouches du Rhône
> 21st June, 1981

Dear Sir,

I have recently returned to Europe after four years' travel and study in India, Burma and Nepal, during which one of my teachers introduced me to your marvellous edition of the *Biographia Mystica* of Meister Sternwärts. It was a complete revelation to me and, together with the *Illuminatum*, has radically changed my whole outlook on life. '*The truly aimed shaft strikes him who looses it*' (Ill. XXIV)!!

I could not permit myself to quit Europe and return home to Chicago without having made an effort to thank you in person and, perhaps, to give myself the treat of conversing with you about the life and works of the Meister.

If you could possibly see your way towards gratifying my wish sometime – say within the next month or so? – would you be so good as to drop me a line at the above address and I will come with all speed to Hautaire.

Yours most sincerely,
J. S. Harland

Spindrift concluded his reading, raised his head and blinked out over the valley. '*Quis Custodiet?*' he murmured, remembering suddenly, with quite astonishing clarity, how once, long ago, Brother Roderigo had handed him a cup of ice-cool water and had then nodded his head in affirmation. How had *he* known?

Hurtling out of the northern sky, three black planes, shaped like assegais, rushed down the length of the valley drowning it with their reverberating thunder. Spindrift sighed, refolded the letter and fumbled it back into its envelope. He reached out, plucked a leaf of wild sage, rubbed it between finger and thumb and held it under his nose. By then the planes were already fifty miles away, skimming low over the distant, glittering sea, but the ripples of their bullying passage still lapped faintly back and forth between the ancient hills.

'Very well,' murmured Spindrift, 'I will write to this young man. *Ex nihilo, nihil fit.* But perhaps Mr Harland is not "nothing". Perhaps he is something – even, maybe, my own successor as I was Roderigo's and Roderigo was Brother Martin's. There always has *been* a successor – a watcher – an eye for the eye.' He grunted, heaved himself up from the grave on which he was sitting and shuffled off towards the Abbey, a slightly dotty old lay brother, muttering to himself as he went.

The counter clerk at the Bureau des Postes sniffed down her nose, glared at the passport which was held out to her and then, reluctantly, handed over the letter, expressing by every means at her disposal short of human speech her profound disapproval of the younger generation.

The slim, deeply tanned, blonde girl in the faded blue shirt and jeans examined the postmark on the letter and chuckled delightedly. She hurried out into the sunny square, sat herself down on a low wall, carefully tore off a narrow strip from the end of the envelope and extracted Spindrift's letter. Her sea-blue eyes flickered rapidly along the lines of typescript. 'Oh *great!*' she exclaimed. 'Gee, isn't that *mar*vellous?'

Judy Harland who, in her twenty-second year, still contrived to look a youthful and boyish eighteen, had once written on some application form in the space reserved for 'Occupation' the single word 'Enthusiast'. They had not offered her the job but it can hardly have been on grounds of self-misrepresentation. Her letter to Spindrift had been dashed off on the spur of the moment when she had discovered that the Abbey of Hautaire was an easy day's hitch-hike down the coast from Arles. Not that the information which she had given Spindrift was untrue – it *was* true – up to a point: that point being that her interest in Meister Sternwärts was but one of several such enthusiasms among which, over the past eight years, she had zoomed back and forth like a tipsy hummingbird in a frangipani forest. She had already sampled Hatha Yoga, the teachings of Don Carlos, Tarot, Zen Buddhism and the 'I-Ching'. Each had possessed her like an ardent lover to the exclusion of all the others – until the next. The *Illuminatum* and the *Biographia Mystica* represented but the most recent of her spiritual love affairs.

Her signing of her letter with her initials rather than her Christian name had been an act of prudence induced by certain awkward experiences in Persia and Afghanistan. She had survived these unscathed, just as she had survived everything else, because her essential self was hedged about by an inviolable conviction that she had been chosen to fulfil some stupendous but as yet unspecified purpose. The fact that she had no very clear idea of what the purpose might be was immaterial. What counted was the strength of the conviction. Indeed, in certain respects, Judy had more than a little in common with Joan of Arc.

A little deft work on her hair with a pair of scissors and a concealed chiffon scarf wound round her chest soon transformed her outwardly into a very passable boy. It was as James Harland that she climbed down from the cab of the friendly *camion* driver, shouldered her well-worn rucksack and strode off, whistling like a bird, up the winding, dusty road towards Hautaire. Just as Spindrift himself had done some sixty years before, and at precisely the same spot, she paused as she came within sight of the Abbey and stood still for a moment, staring up at it. She saw a brown and white eagle corkscrewing majestically upwards in an invisible funnel of warm air and, as she watched it, she experienced an almost overwhelming impulse to turn round and go back. Perhaps if she had been under the aegis of the 'I-Ching' she would have obeyed it, but Hautaire was now to her what fabled Cathay had once been to Peter Sternwärts – a challenge to be met and overcome. Shrugging aside her forebodings she hooked her thumbs more firmly under the straps of her pack and marched on up the road.

Old age had lengthened Spindrift's vision. From the library window he had picked out the determined little figure when it was still three-quarters of a mile away. Something about it touched his heart like a cold finger. '*Golden-haired like an angel.*' Had he not himself written that long, long ago, after his last visit to the rotunda? How many years was it now? Fifty at least. As far as the eye could see. Why then had he not gone back? Was it fear? Or lack of any real religious faith to sustain him? Yet everything he had 'seen' had come to pass just as he had described it. Such crazy things they had seemed too. Sunburst bombs shattering whole cities in the blink of an eye; men in silver suits walking on the face of the moon; an assassin's bullets striking down the President who would put them there; the endless wars; the horror and anguish of the extermination camps; human bestiality. Pain, pain, always pain. Until he had been able to endure no more. His last entry in the *Praemonitiones* must be almost due now. Did that mean he had failed in his bounden duty? Well, then, so he had failed, but at least he had given the world the *Biographia* and none of his predecessors had done that. And there was still the marvel of the *Exploratio Spiritualis* to come – that masterpiece which he alone had unearthed, translated, and pieced together. Perhaps one day it would be published. But not by him. Let someone else shoulder that burden. He knew what it would entail. And surely he had done enough. But the chill lay there in his heart like a splinter of ice that would not melt. '*Golden-haired like an angel.*' Muttering to himself he turned away from the window, shuffled across the library and began making his way down to the Abbey gate to greet his visitor.

As a child Judy had sometimes toyed with a fanciful notion that people grew to resemble the names they had been born with. She was reminded of it when she first set eyes on Spindrift. His hair was as white and soft as the wisps of foam on a weir-pool and he blinked at her waterily through his steel-rimmed glasses as he shook her by the hand. 'You are very young, Mr Harland,' he observed. 'But then, to you I dare say I must seem very old.'

'Are you?' she asked in that blunt way of hers which some people found charming and others simply ill-mannered.

'I am exactly as old as this century,' he replied with a smile. 'Which makes me four score and one. A goodly stretch by any reckoning, wouldn't you say?'

'And you've lived here all your life?'

'Most of it, to be sure. I first came to Hautaire in 1923.'

'Hey! My *father* was born in 1923!'

'An *annus mirabilis*, indeed,' the old man chuckled. 'Come

along, Mr Harland. Let me be the first to introduce you to Hautaire.'

So saying he led her through the outer courtyard and down into the cloisters where, like ghostly autumnal leaves, a few of the brothers were wandering in silent meditation. Judy's bright magpie glance darted this way and that. 'Say,' she whispered, 'this sure is some place.'

'Would you care for a drink?' asked Spindrift, suddenly recalling his own introduction to the Abbey and hoping, vaguely, that by repeating the pattern he would be vouchsafed a sign of some kind.

'I surely would,' said Judy. 'Thanks a lot.' She shrugged off her rucksack and dumped it down beside the basin of the fountain while Spindrift groped around short-sightedly for the cup.

'Here, let me,' she said and, scooping up the cup, she dipped it into the basin and took a hearty swig.

Spindrift adjusted his spectacles and peered at her. A solitary drop of water hung for a moment like a tear from her square firm chin and then she had brushed it away with the back of her hand. 'That was great,' she informed him. 'Real cool.'

Spindrift nodded and smiled. 'That fountain was here even before the Abbey was built,' he said.

'Is that so? Then Meister Sternwärts may have done just what I've done.'

'Yes,' agreed Spindrift. 'It is more than likely.'

'That's really something,' sighed Judy. 'Hey, I've brought my copy of the *Biographia* for you to autograph. It's right here in my pack. I carry it around every place I go.'

'Oh, really?' said Spindrift, flushing with pleasure. 'I must say I regard that as a great compliment.'

'The *Biographia*'s one of the world's great books,' averred Judy stoutly. 'Possibly the greatest.'

Spindrift felt appropriately flattered. 'Perhaps you would be interested to see the original manuscript?' he suggested diffidently.

'*Would* I! You mean you have it right here in the Abbey?'

'It's in the library.'

'Well, what are we waiting for?' demanded Judy. 'I mean – that is – if it's convenient.'

'Oh, yes, yes,' Spindrift assured her. 'We'll just call in at the guest wing first and I'll show you your quarters. We can go straight on up from there.'

Judy's unfeigned enthusiasm for the Meister was all the old man could have wished for. He laid out the original manuscript of the *Biographia Mystica* before her and guided her through it while she gave little gasps and exclamations of wonder and pleasure. 'It's just as if you'd known him personally, Mr Spindrift,' she said at last. 'You make him come alive.'

'Oh, he *is*, Mr Harland. It is a gross error on our part to assume that life is mere physical existence. The *élan vital* lives on in the sublime creations of human genius. One only needs to study the *Exploratio Spiritualis* to realize that.'

'And what's the *Exploratio Spiritualis*, Mr Spindrift?'

'One day, I hope, it will be recognized as the *Biographia Mystica* of the human mind.'

'You don't say?'

'But I *do*, Mr Harland. And, what is more, I have the best of reasons for saying so.'

Judy looked up at him curiously. 'You don't mean that you've dug up *another* work by Meister Sternwärts?'

Spindrift nodded emphatically.

'Why that's marvellous!' she cried. 'Sensational! Can I see it?'

'It would mean very little to you, I'm afraid, Mr Harland. The *Spiritualis* was written in cipher.'

'And you've cracked it? Translated it?'

'I have.'

'Wow!' breathed Judy.

'I have spent the last twenty-five years working at it,' said Spindrift, with more than a trace of pride in his voice. 'It is, I might pardonably claim, my swan-song.'

'And when's it going to be published?'

'By me – never.'

'But why on earth not?'

'The responsibility is too great.'

'How do you mean?'

Spindrift lifted his head and gazed out of the open library window towards the distant invisible sea. 'The world is not yet ready for the *Spiritualis*,' he murmured. 'Peter realized that, which is why he chose to write it in the form he did.'

Judy frowned. 'I'm afraid I'm still not with you, Mr Spindrift. Why isn't it ready?'

'To accept a determinist universe as a proven fact?'

'Who says we're not?'

Almost reluctantly Spindrift withdrew his gaze from the far horizon and blinked down at her. 'You mean you *can* accept it, Mr Harland?' he asked curiously.

'Well, I certainly accept the "I-Ching".'

'But you must, surely, believe in free will?'

'Well, up to a point, sure I do. I mean to say *I* have to consult the "I-Ching". It doesn't decide *for* me that I'm going to consult it, does it?'

It seemed to Spindrift at that moment that he had reached the final cross-roads. But he was still not sure which path was the right one. He stirred the air vaguely with his fingers. 'Then tell me, Mr Harland,' he said, 'for the sake of the supposition, if you wish – what do you suppose would follow if one succeeded in convincing the human race that everything in life *was* pre-ordained?'

Judy smiled. 'But most of them believe it anyway. Astrology; Tarot: "I-Ching" – you name it; we'll believe it. The fault, Mr Spindrift, lies not in our selves but in our stars.'

'Really?' said Spindrift. 'I must say that you astonish me.'

'Well, a lot's happened in the last thirty years. We're the post H-Bomb generation, remember. We got to see where reason had led us. Right bang up to the edge of the precipice.'

Spindrift nodded. 'Yes, yes,' he murmured. 'I know. I saw it.'

'Come again?'

'The *Pikadon*. That's what they called it.' He closed his eyes and shuddered. A moment later he had gripped her by the arm. 'But imagine *knowing* that was going to happen and that you were powerless to prevent it. What then, Mr Harland?'

'How do you mean "knowing"?'

'Just that,' Spindrift insisted. 'Seeing it all happening *before* it *had* happened. Years and years before. What then?'

'Are you serious?'

'It's all there in the *Spiritualis*,' said Spindrift, releasing his hold on her arm and gripping the back of her chair with both hands. 'Peter Sternwärts rediscovered what Apollonius of Tyana had brought back with him from the East. But he did

31

more than that. He devised the means whereby this knowledge could be handed down to future generations. He was a seer who bequeathed his eyes to posterity.'

Judy's eyes narrowed. 'Just let me get this straight,' she said slowly. 'Are you telling me that Meister Sternwärts could actually *see* the future?'

'Yes,' said Spindrift simply.

'What? *All* of it?'

'No. Only the biggest storms on the horizon – the crises for civilization. He called them "Knots in Time".'

'But how do you know that?'

'He wrote them down,' said Spindrift. 'In a book he called *Praemonitiones.*'

'Holy Moses!' Judy whispered. 'You just *have* to be kidding!'

'Sternwärts' own forecasts extend only as far as the fifteenth century, but, as I said before, he bequeathed his eyes to posterity.'

'And just what does that *mean*, Mr Spindrift?'

Spindrift drew in his breath. 'Wait here a moment, Mr Harland,' he said, 'and I will do my best to show you what it means.'

A minute later he was back carrying the first volume of the *Praemonitiones.* He opened it at the frontispiece map and spread it out before her. Then he settled his spectacles firmly on his nose and began to explain what was what.

'This was drawn by Peter Sternwärts himself,' he said. 'There can be no question of that. It represents a bird's-eye view of the area within which Hautaire is situated. These dots represent the Neolithic stone circle and the straight lines radiating from the menhirs all cross at this point here. I thought at first that these spirals were some primitive attempt to represent lines of magnetic force but I know now that this is not so. Nevertheless, they do represent a force field of some kind – one, moreover, which was undoubtedly first detected by the ancient race who raised the original stone circle. Sternwärts realized that the menhirs acted as some sort of focusing device and that the area of maximum intensity would probably occur at the point where the intersection of the chords was held in equilibrium by the force field – what he called the *mare temporis* – sea of time.'

Judy nodded. 'So?' she said.

'He deduced that at this particular point he would find what he was seeking. I have since unearthed among the archives a number of sketches he made of similar stone circles in Brittany. And just off the centre of each he has written the same word *oculus* – that is the Latin word for "eye".'

'Hey,' said Judy, 'you don't mean . . .'

'Indeed I do,' insisted Spindrift. 'After an immense amount of trial and error he succeeded in locating the precise point – and it is a very small area indeed – right here in Hautaire itself. Having found it he built himself a time observatory and then proceeded to set down on record everything he saw. The results are there before you. The *Praemonitiones*!'

Judy stared down at the map. 'But if that's so, why hasn't anyone else discovered one? I mean there's Stonehenge and Carnac and so forth, isn't there?'

Spindrift nodded. 'That mystified Peter too, until he realized that the focal point of each circle was almost invariably situated a good twenty or so metres above ground level. He postulates that in the days when the circles were first raised, wooden towers were erected in their centres. The seer, who would probably have been a high priest, would have had sole access to that tower. In the case of Hautaire it just so happened that the site of the long-vanished tower was occupied by the rotunda of the Abbey.'

'And that was why Sternwärts came here?'

'No, Peter came to Hautaire because he had reason to believe that Apollonius of Tyana had made a special point of visiting this particular circle. There was apparently still a pagan shrine and a resident oracle here in the first century AD.'

Judy turned over some pages in the book before her but she barely glanced at what was written there. 'But how does it *work*?' she asked. 'What do you do in this *oculus*? Peek into a crystal ball or something?'

'One sees,' said Spindrift vaguely. 'Within the mind's eye.'

'But *how*?'

'That I have never discovered. Nor, I hazard, did Peter. Nevertheless that is what happens.'

'And can you choose what you want to see?'

'I used to think not,' said Spindrift, 'but since I stumbled upon the key to the *Exploratio Spiritualis* I have been forced to revise my opinion. I now believe that Peter Sternwärts was deliberately working towards the goal of a spiritual and mental discipline which would allow him to exert a direct influence upon

33

what he saw. His aim was to become a shaper of the future as well as a seer.'

Judy's blue eyes widened perceptibly. 'A *shaper*?' she echoed. 'And did he?'

'It is impossible to tell,' said Spindrift. 'But it is surely not without significance that he left Hautaire before he died.'

'Come again?'

'Well, by the time he left he knew for certain that chance does nothing that has not been prepared well in advance. He must have realized that the only way in which he could exert an influence upon the future would be by acting in the present. If he could succeed in tracing the thread backwards from its knot he might be able to step in and adjust things at the very point where only the merest modicum of intervention could affect the future. Of course, you must understand that this is all the purest supposition on my part.'

Judy nodded. 'And these disciplines – mental whatsits – what were they?'

'They were expressly designed to enable the seer to select his own particular vision. Having seen the catastrophe ahead he could, if he were successful, feel his way backwards in time from that point and, hopefully, reach a *junctura criticalis* – the precise germinal instant of which some far-off tragedy was the progeny.'

'Yes, I understand that. But what *sort* of disciplines were they?'

'Ironically, Mr Harland, they appear to have had a good deal in common with those which are still practised today among certain Eastern faiths.'

'What's ironical about that?'

'Well, surely, the avowed aim of the Oriental sages is to achieve the ultimate annihilation of the self – of the ego. What Peter Sternwärts was hoping to achieve seems to me to have been the exact opposite – the veritable apotheosis of the human ego! Nothing less than the elevation of Man to God! He had a persistent vision of himself as the potter and the whole of humanity as his clay. That explains why, throughout the *Exploratio*, he constantly refers to himself as a "shaper". It also explains why I have shunned the responsibility of publishing it.'

'Then why are you telling me?' demanded Judy shrewdly.

Spindrift removed his spectacles, closed his eyes, and massaged his eyelids with his fingertips. 'I am very old, Mr Harland,' he said at last. 'It is now over fifty years since I last visited the *oculus* and the world is very close to the horizon of my own visions. Ever since Abbé Ferrand's untimely death forty years ago the secret of the *oculus* has been mine alone. If I were to die this minute it would perish with me and I, by default, would have betrayed the trust which I believe has been reposed in me. In other words I would die betraying the very man who has meant far more to me than any I have ever known in the flesh – Peter Sternwärts himself.'

'But why choose *me*?' Judy insisted. 'Why not one of the other brothers?'

Spindrift sighed. 'I think, Mr Harland, that it is perhaps because I recognize in you some of my own lifelong reverence for Peter Sternwärts. Furthermore, in some manner which I find quite impossible to explain, I am convinced that you are associated with the last visit I paid to the *oculus* – with my final vision.'

'Really? And what was that?'

Spindrift looked down at the parchment which had absorbed so much of his life, and then he shook his head. 'There was a girl,' he murmured. 'A girl with golden hair . . .'

'A *girl*?'

Like a waterlogged corpse rising slowly to the surface the old man seemed to float up from the trouble depths of some dark and private nightmare. His eyes cleared. 'Why, yes,' he said. 'A *girl*. Do you know, Mr Harland, in all these years that point had never struck me before! A girl, *here in Hautaire*!' He began to chuckle wheezily. 'Oh dear, oh dear, oh dear! Why that would be the end of the world indeed!'

In spite of herself Judy was deeply moved by the old man's transparent relief. Instinctively she put out her hand and laid it on his. 'I don't know what your vision was, Mr Spindrift,' she said. 'But if you feel I can be of help to you in any way . . .'

Spindrift brought his other hand across and patted hers abstractedly. 'That is most kind of you, Mr Harland,' he murmured. 'Really, most kind . . .'

At supper that evening the Abbot stepped up to the lectern in the refectory and raised a hand for silence. The murmur of voices stilled as the brothers turned their wondering eyes towards their Father Superior. He surveyed them all in silence for a long moment and then said: 'Brethren and honoured guests ... my friends. Here at Hautaire we live a life whose fundamental pattern was laid down for us more than a thousand years ago. I believe it is a good life, one which has accordingly found favour in the eyes of God. My cherished hope is that a thousand years from now its pattern will have remained, in all essential respects, as it is today – that the spiritual verities enshrined in our Foundation will be what they have always been – a source of comfort and reassurance to all God-loving men; a harbour of hope and tranquillity in a storm-tossed world.'

He paused as though uncertain how to continue and they all saw him close his eyes and turn his face upwards in mute prayer for a long, long minute. When at last he looked down upon them again the silence in the hall was almost palpable.

'My friends, I have just learnt that certain European powers, acting in concert with Israel and the United States of America, have this afternoon launched an armed invasion of Saudi Arabia and the Trucial States.'

There was a concerted gasp of horror and a sudden burst of whispering. The Abbot raised his voice to carry over the hubbub.

'Their avowed aim is to secure for themselves access to the oil supplies which they deem essential to their national, political and economic survival. Under the terms of the Baghdad Treaty of 1979, the Arabs have called upon the Soviet Union for immediate armed assistance, and Russia and its allies have demanded the instant and total withdrawal of the invading forces. Failure to comply with this demand will, they say, bring about inevitable consequences.'

He paused again and regarded them sombrely. 'I shall personally conduct a service for Divine Intercession immediately after Compline. It will be held in the Main Chapel. It goes without saying that all our guests are invited to attend. *Dominus Vobiscum.*' He sketched the sign of the Cross over them, stepped down from the lectern, and strode swiftly out of the hall.

In the outburst of chattering which erupted immediately the Abbot had left the hall Spindrift turned to Judy and seized her by the arm. 'You must come with me, Mr Harland,' he whispered urgently. 'At once.'

Judy, who was still groping to come to terms with all the

36

implications of what she had heard, nodded submissively and allowed the old man to shepherd her out of the refectory and up into the library. He unearthed the keys to the *oculus* and the rotunda then hurried her up the stairs and along the deserted passages to the door which had remained locked for more than half a century. He was possessed by an almost feverish impatience and kept up an incessant muttering to himself the whole way. Judy could hardly make out a word of what he was saying, but more than once she thought she caught the strange word '*Pikadon*'. It meant nothing to her at all.

So much rubbish had accumulated in the narrow passage that they had to lean their combined weight against the rotunda door before they managed to force it open. They squeezed through into the crevasse beyond and Spindrift lit a candle he had brought with him. By its wavering light the two of them scuffled their way forward to the *oculus*.

When they reached it Spindrift handed the key to Judy and held the candle so that she could see what she was doing. A minute later the door had creaked open to expose the sarcophagus, standing just as it had stood for the last seven hundred years.

Judy gaped at it in astonishment. 'You mean you go in *there*?'

'*You* must, Mr Harland,' said Spindrift. 'Please hurry.'

'But *why*?' demanded Judy. 'What's the point? What good could it do?'

Spindrift gripped her by the shoulder and almost succeeded in thrusting her bodily into the casque. 'Don't you understand, Mr Harland?' he cried. 'It is *you* who must prove my final vision false! *You have to prove me wrong!!*'

Into her twenty-two years of life Judy had already packed more unusual experiences than had most women three times her age, but none of them had prepared her for this. Alone with a looney octogenarian who seemed bent on stuffing her into a stone coffin buried somewhere inside the walls of a medieval monastery! For all she knew, once he had got her inside he would turn the key on her and leave her there to rot. And yet, at the very moment when she most needed her physical strength it had apparently deserted her. Her arms, braced against the stone slabs, seemed all but nerveless, her legs so weak she wondered if they were not going to fold under her. 'The key,' she muttered. 'Give me the key. And you go away. Right away. Back to that other door. You can wait for me there.'

The pressure of Spindrift's hand relaxed. Judy stepped back and fumbled the key out of the lock. Then, feeling a little more confident, she turned to face the old man. By the trembling light of the candle she glimpsed the streaks of tears on his ancient cheeks. 'Please go, Mr Spindrift,' she pleaded. '*Please*.'

'But you will do it?' he begged. 'I must *know*, Mr Harland.'

'Yes, yes,' she said. 'Sure I will. I give you my word.'

He shuffled backwards a few doubtful paces and stood watching her. 'Would you like me to leave you the candle?' he asked.

'All right,' she said. 'Put it down there on the floor.'

She waited until he had done it and then, aloud, she started to count slowly up to sixty. She had reached barely half way before the rotunda was buffeted by the massive reverberating thunder of war planes hurtling past high overhead. Judy shivered violently and, without bothering to finish her count, stepped the two short paces back into the casque until her shoulders were pressed against the cold stone. 'Please, dear God,' she whispered, 'let it be all—'

She was falling, dropping vertically downwards into the bowels of the earth as if down the shaft of an elevator. Yet the candle, still standing there before her just where the old man had left it and burning with its quiet golden flame, told her that her stomach lied. But her sense of vertigo was so acute that she braced her arms against the sides of the coffin in an effort to steady herself. Watery saliva poured into her mouth. Certain she was about to faint she swallowed and closed her eyes.

Like magenta fire balloons the after-images of the candleflame drifted across her retinas. They changed imperceptibly to green, to dark blue, to purple and finally vanished into the velvety darkness. Her eyelids felt as though lead weights had been laid upon them.

Suddenly – without warning of any kind – she found herself gazing down, as if from a great height, upon a city. With the instant familiarity bred of a dozen High School civics assignments, she knew it at once for her own home town. The whole panoramic scene had a strange, almost dream-like clarity. The air was unbelievably clear, no trace of smoke or haze obscured the uncompromising grid of the streets. Northwards Lake Michigan glittered silver-blue in the bright sunshine while the plum-blue shadows of drifting clouds ghosted silently across its placid waters. But this was no longer the Chicago she remembered. The whole centre of the metropolis was gone. Where it had been was nothing but a vast circular smudge of grey rubble, along the fringes of which green shrubs were already growing. No factory stacks smoked; no glittering lines of automobiles choked these expressways; no freight trains wriggled and jinked through these latticed sidings; all was as dead and as still as a city on the moon. This was indeed Necropolis, City of the Dead.

At last the vision faded and its place was taken by another. She now found herself gazing out across a vast plain through which wound a great river. But the endless golden Danubian wheatfields which she remembered so well had all vanished. The winds which sent the towering cloud schooners scudding across this sky blew only through the feathered heads of weeds and wild grasses which stretched out like a green and rippling sea to the world's end. Of man, or cattle, or even flying bird there was no sign at all.

One after another the visions came and went and it was almost as if the *oculus* itself were searching desperately for some sign of the vanished race that had devised it and given it its purpose. Like a forlorn radar beacon it swept out into the world of the future and found no trace of man at all.

When Spindrift returned some twenty minutes later, it was to discover Judy crouched in the bottom of the sarcophagus, curled up like a dormouse with her head resting on her bent knees. Fearfully he stooped over her and placed his hand on her shoulder. 'Mr Harland,' he whispered urgently. 'Mr Harland, are you all right?'

There was no response. He knelt down, thrust his hands beneath her arms and, by a mighty effort, succeeded in dragging her clear of the casque. She flopped sideways against the door then sprawled forwards beside him. He fumbled his hand inside the neck of her shirt, felt for the beating of her heart, and so discovered who she was. The last dim flicker of hope died within him.

He patted her deathly cheeks and chafed her hands until at last her eyelids fluttered open. 'What happened?' he asked. 'What did you see?'

She raised a cold hand and wonderingly touched his wrinkled

face with her fingertips. 'Then it *hasn't* happened,' she whispered. 'And it was *so* real.'

'It *will* happen,' he said sadly. 'Whatever it was you saw must come to pass. It always has.'

'But there was no one,' she mourned. 'No one at all. What happened, Mr Spindrift? Where had they all gone?'

'Come, my dear,' he urged, gently coaxing her to her feet. 'Come with me.'

The air on the hillside was still warm, drowsy with the summer scents of wild sage, lavender and rosemary, as the old man and the girl made their way up the dim path towards the ridge where the ancient neoliths still bared themselves like broken teeth against the night sky. Below them the Abbey lights glowed out cheerfully and small figures could be seen moving back and forth behind the chapel windows.

They reached a point where an outcrop of limestone had been roughly shaped into a seat. Spindrift eased himself on to it, drew Judy down beside him and spread out the wide skirt of his habit to cover her. As he did so he could feel her trembling like a crystal bell that, once struck, goes on quivering far below the threshold of audible sound. An enormous, impotent grief seized him by the throat. Too late he saw what he should have done, how he had betrayed the trust that Brother Roderigo and the Abbé Ferrand had laid upon him. But he saw too, with a sort of numb clarity, how he, Spindrift, could not have done it because, within himself, some vital spark of faith in humanity had been extinguished far back in the blood-stained ruins of 1917. He could no longer believe that men were essentially good, or that the miracle which the genius of Peter Sternwärts had created would not be used in some hideous way to further the purposes of evil.

Yet what if he *had* gone that one step further; *had* published the *Exploratio Spiritualis* and given to all men the means of foreseeing the inevitable consequences of their insane greed, their overweening arrogance, their atavistic lust for power? Who was to say that Armageddon might not have been averted; that Peter's miracle might not have succeeded in shaping anew the human spirit? *Quis custodiet ipsos custodes?* Ah, who indeed, if not God? And Spindrift's God had died in the mud of Ypres.

The full knowledge of what he had done rose as bitter as bile at the back of the old man's throat. Desperately he sought for some words of comfort for the girl who crouched beside him and could not stop shivering. Some lie; some little harmless lie. 'I did not tell you before,' he said, 'but I believe you are destined to publish the *Spiritualis* for me. Yes, I remember now. That was how you were to be associated with my final vision. So you see, there *is* still hope.'

But even as he spoke the distant eastern horizon suddenly flickered as though with summer lightning. His arm tightened involuntarily around the girl's shoulders. She stirred. 'O God,' she moaned softly. 'O God, O God, O God.' A harsh, grating sob shook her, and then another and another.

A second flash threw the low clouds into sharp relief and, a moment later, the whole arching roof of the world was lit up like the day. An urgent bell began tolling in the Abbey.

Something scratched a line like a blood-red stalk high up into the southern sky and a ball of blue-white fire blossomed in strange and sinister silence.

And later a wind began to blow from the north.

Paradise Beach

'Who?' demanded the voice from the So-Vi speaker, while the features on the screen contorted themselves into a parody of amused incredulity. '*Ketchup?*'

'Ket*skoff*. Igor Ketskoff. Don't say you've never *heard* of him, Margot.'

'I've never heard of him,' said the face on the screen, and laughed. Then, relenting, asked: 'What does he *do* exactly, Zeph?'

'*Trompe l'oeil* illusions. Murals. *You* know.'

'Oh. Like Rex Whistler, you mean?'

'Not a bit like Rex Whistler. Well, maybe a *tiny* bit. Igor uses – hang on, I've got it here somewhere – "micro-miniaturized, solid-state, depth fluorescence technology to create his modern miracles of multi-dimensional anamorphosis".'

'Ana – *what?*'

'Morphosis. That's what it says here, anyway.'

'What's it mean?'

'*I* don't know. Illusion, I suppose. Anyway, Margot, the point is he's doing one for us.'

'"Us"? You mean Hugo's *agreed*?'

'Hugo com*missioned* it! Igor's under contract to some weird little outfit called *Artefax*. S & L got them as part of a blanket take-over in February. When Hugo got round to sorting things out and weeding out what they didn't want he stumbled across *Artefax* and Igor.'

'*I see*. Still, I must confess I'm a bit surprised, Zeph. I mean I've never thought of Sir Hugo as a patron of the fine arts exactly.'

'Between the two of us, sweetie, he sees it more in the nature of an investment. By the way, you're invited to the private view on the tenth.'

'Ah! Now I'm getting warmer! All Hugo's tame tycoons assemble to gawp then rush back to Lombard Street and order an Igor ana-whatsit to grace their board-rooms. *Artefax* shares go into orbit and Sherwood and Lazarus, Merchant Bankers, stagger home with the loot. Right?'

'What a cynical girl you are, Margot.'

'I know. It's all part of my charm, Zeph.'

Zephyr Sherwood laughed. 'The tenth, then. Seven thirty. And don't forget.'

'Try keeping me away.'

The gathering which assembled in Astral Court, W.1. for Sir Hugo and Lady Sherwood's private view contained at least five ex-lovers of Zephyr's and a fair cross-section of the merchant banking fraternity. Margot Brierly coolly appraised the combined capital resources of a mere half dozen guests as being, by 1992 standards, well on the upward slope of five million New Pounds – that is to say five hundred million in Old Sterling. She found the knowledge lent them a charm they would otherwise have lacked. Fortunately, Zephyr had seen fit to leaven the dough with a lavish sprinkling of talents chosen from among her numerous friends and acquaintances. Margot recognized three So-Vi stars, a *very* striking transvestite who ran a syndicated trans-European fashion column, and a remarkably hairy young footballer who, she recalled, had recently been transferred from one club to another for a record-breaking fee. (Could *he* be Zephyr's latest?)

Extricating herself from the predatory tendrils of a lesser Lombard Street gnome Margot wriggled her way through the throng to where Zephyr was holding court swinging gently to and fro from a rococo *balançoire*. Having restrained her friend in mid-swoop Margot said: 'Well, come on. Which is he, dear?'

'Which is who?'

'Igor Thingummy, of course.'

Zephyr beckoned to the preambulating auto-butler, exchanged her empty champagne glass for a full one from the proffered tray and gestured with a bejewelled hand towards a knot of guests among whom Margot recognized only Sir Hugo Sherwood. 'Iggy's the little pet with the moustache,' said Zephyr. 'Isn't he a dink?'

The little pet in question chose that moment to glance towards his hostess. His teeth flashed like a space beacon. In response to Zephyr's fluttered fingers he came scuttling across to her side.

'Iggy, I want you to meet Margot Brierly,' said Zephyr. 'She writes those *fabulously* intelligent detective stories.'

'Enchanté,' said Igor, clicking his heels and bowing from the waist with clockwork precision. He straightened and eyed Margot caressingly up and down. 'Ah,' he breathed, 'but *you* I could im*mortalize*, madame!'

Margot restrained an impulse to feel if her dress was still fastened and smiled ingenuously. 'I've been wanting to ask you what anamorphosis is, Mr . . .'

'Ketskoff,' grinned Zephyr. 'Rhymes with Ketskoff.'

'Oh, that is simple enough,' said Igor airily. 'The word itself is derived from the Greek. It means "to change the form of". The artists of the Renaissance discovered that by copying faithfully the reflection which they saw in a distorting mirror they could, as it were, encode a vision. Their vision could only be *de*-coded by placing before it a similar mirror to that in which they had first viewed the original reflection.'

'Like that picture by Holbein in the N.G.?' said Margot brightly. 'You know the one – with the two men and the lute.'

'*The Ambassadors*, madame,' said Igor, obviously rather impressed. 'However, I use the term in a somewhat less restricted sense. The mirror *I* employ is nothing less than the psycho-kinetic field of the observer himself. No two people see precisely the same Ketskoff. The modulations are infinite and infinitely subtle.'

'And infinitely expensive?'

'They are not cheap, certainly. But then you must remember that each one is individually styled and structured round its owner's personal psycho-emotive threshold. That demands considerable technical finesse.'

'If you're ready, Igor?' Sir Hugo hove up alongside Zephyr's swing, beamed blandly at Margot and raised an interrogative eyebrow.

'Everything is in order, Sir Hugo. I have arranged for the main lighting to be subdued just before we switch on.'

'Excellent. I'll shepherd them down, say my few words and leave the rest to you.' The banker consulted his wristwatch. 'Kick off in five minutes from now?'

Igor nodded, bowed briefly to Margot and Zephyr and scurried away down the shallow flight of stairs to the mezzanine where one long wall was concealed from view behind heavy, plum-coloured velvet drapes.

'Well, what do you make of him?' inquired Zephyr.

'I'm not sure,' said Margot pensively. 'I think I detect something a shade spooky.'

'Little Iggy, *spooky*? For heaven's sake! He's just a pet.'

'House trained?'

Zephyr tinkled a laugh. 'Come on,' she said. 'If we want the best view we'd better get downstairs.'

Sir Hugo's speech was brief and to the point. For 150 years, ever since the invention of the camera, pictorial art and scientific technology had been struggling to come to terms with one another, though without notable success. Theirs had been a genuine love/hate relationship in which both strove for domination. Fundamental to the artists' deep distrust was the realization that what the machine had created once it could create again and again, whereas the artist's vision was essentially unique. The invention of neo-anamorphics had resolved, once and for all, the ancient dilemma. It was, he sincerely believed, the ultimate artform of the twenty-first century, and Igor Ketskoff would inevitably be ranked with such names as Kandinsky and Picasso. Let those present judge for themselves.

The lights dimmed precipitately to total black-out; there was a gentle purring as the drapes parted; and then, with all the nerve-tingling impact of a lightning flash, illumination flooded out of the wall. There was a concerted gasp from the assembled guests; hands rose to shade dazzled eyes; and then, mingled with cries of: 'Superb!' 'Incredible!' 'Formidable!', spontaneous applause erupted.

To Margot the illusion was, indeed, wholly astonishing. It was exactly as if an area some 5 metres by 2 metres had been removed bodily from the penthouse wall and replaced by an unglazed window which looked upon a curving Caribbean beach. To the left, tall, feathery palms rustled in the gentlest of breezes, dappling a carpet of dusky shadow as they receded into the eye-aching distance along the silver-white margin of the cove. Pellucid wavelets gambolled in to subside like sleepy kittens on the gently shelving sand. Far out to sea a line of twinkling spray marked where the submerged reef was absorbing the force of the Atlantic rollers. As illusion it was perfect – *too* perfect! It *had* to be real!

Moving hesitantly forward, Margot stretched out her hand and felt – nothing at all! It was exactly as if, at the moment of contact with the invisible barrier which separated her hand from the sandy shore she could see so clearly, all physical sensation was short-circuited, and the reassuring messages no longer flowed through the nerve-endings in her fingertips to her brain. She felt totally disorientated, closed her eyes and stepped backwards. Had she been a cat every single hair on her body would have been standing upright. She shivered so violently that she all but dropped the glass she was holding.

'Well,' murmured Zephyr, 'I think we rate this one a genuine *tour de force*, don't you?'

Margot nodded. 'Where is it supposed to be?' she asked.

'Paradise Beach, Grenada. Hey, just get an eyeful of *that*!'

Margot turned again to the panorama. The glittering sand ribboned out and rippled away into the azure distance, remote and calm and beautiful. 'An eyeful of what?' she asked.

Zephyr was staring fixedly at a point somewhere in the left foreground. On her face was an expression of almost envious curiosity. 'Well, I'll be damned,' she murmured.

'What is it?' Margot insisted.

'Those two,' hissed Zephyr. 'Hey, he's *all* man, isn't he?'

Margot screwed up her eyes and saw only a foraging spider-crab scuttling sideways across the distant strand. 'What are you talking about?' she said. 'Who's "all man"'?

A flush like a faint fingerprint coloured Zephyr's cheeks. Her eyes sparkled. 'Wow!' she whispered, and again: '*Wow!*'

Margot glanced rapidly round at the other guests. Several of them appeared to be staring as if hypnotized by one point or another of the anamorphic. At that moment a familiar voice breathed in her ear: 'Is it not as I said, *madame*? No two people see exactly the same Ketskoff.'

She jerked round to find Igor smirking at her. 'But what *are* they seeing?' she demanded.

Igor shrugged. 'Why ask me? I supply only the canvas and the frame. They paint their own pictures.'

'And how about Sir Hugo? I mean, after all, it's *his*, isn't it?'

'Indeed it is. I have here in my pocket his cheque to prove it.'

'Well, what does *he* get out of it?'

Igor sniggered. 'He reserves to himself the right to play Prospero. After all, *madame*, it is *his* island.' He flashed his teeth at her in a gleaming grin. 'And now it is time for me to see how the fat fish are nibbling.' he whispered. '*Au revoir, chère madame.*'

'Zeph! I've been trying to get hold of you for *weeks*! Where on earth have you been?'

'Brazil, of course. Where else?'

'Why Brazil, for heaven's sake?'

'Oh, come off it, Margot. *Think.*'

'The coffee?'

'The World Cup, you prune.'

'Football? And since when have you . . . *Ah-h-h!*'

The beautiful face on the So-Vi gave a smug, lip-licking grin. 'Oh, it's a great sport, Margot. The greatest.'

'Yes?'

'Well, let's say the second greatest.'

'Did you win?'

'I wasn't *playing*, dear. Just watching. We were knocked out in the semi-final. The ref. had been got at.'

'By you?'

'Ah, if only I'd thought of it!'

'I'm sure you will next time. How's Hugo?'

'Oh, banking away busily as usual. You know Hugo.'

'Zeph, doesn't he *mind*?'

'Mind what?'

'*You* know. Your extra-connubial activities. Ball games and so on.'

'Well, naturally I don't make a point of *discussing* it with him, if that's what you mean.'

'But he must *know*, Zeph.'

'A banker's wife needs her little hobbies, dear.'

'Plural?'

'Oh, most singularly plural,' agreed Zephyr and produced one of those tinkling little laughs of hers which always set Margot's teeth on edge. 'And what have you been up to, sweetie?'

'Scribbling away,' said Margot. 'I've just finished the first draft of another Inspector Calloway. Provisional title: "Quietus in Triplicate".'

'Well done, you. Been to any parties?'

'A couple. Dull to middling. Oh, I bumped into Igor at one of them.'

'Igor Ketskoff?'

'How many Igors do you know, for heaven's sake? He told me he'd got three new commissions. Seemed pretty pleased with himself. How's *Paradise Beach* by the way?'

'Hugo had it moved into his study while I was away. Said it dominated the mezzanine too much. He's probably right.'

'I'm surprised you *can* move them.'

'*Artefax* handled all that. I dare say it cost a bomb though. Hey, before I forget, Margot, are you doing anything on Friday?'

'Friday? No, I don't think so. Nothing I can't put off. Why?'

'Come down to Hickstead with me.'

'*Hickstead!* What on earth for?'

'The show-jumping, idiot.'

'*Show-jumping!* I didn't think you knew one end of a horse from the other.'

'Strictly between us, dear, I still have to think it out. But I met someone in São Paulo who spends most of his daylight hours sitting on the top of one of them.'

'Zeph, you are absolutely *incorrigible*!'

'No, dear, just curious.'

'Margot, are you frantically busy, or can you spare an old friend a few minutes?'

'Hello, Zeph! Where are you calling from?'

'The Continental Club. Fredrico's booked in here for the Royal Show.'

'Fredrico? Oh, yes, I remember. Captain Gonzales. We met at Hickstead, didn't we?'

'That's right. Now listen, Margot. You'd say I was a pretty level-headed type, wouldn't you?'

'Oh, to a fault, dear.'

'Not prone to imagining things?'

'Not since *I've* known you. Why?'

'Well, there's something very odd going on.'

'Odd?'

'I mean I'm quite sure there must *be* a perfectly logical explanation but I just can't think what it is.'

'Explanation of *what*, Zeph?'

'Hugo's behaviour.'

'*Hugo?* What on earth's he been up to?'

'That's just what *I'd* like to know.'

'Just a moment, old thing. Why don't you start at the beginning and put me in the picture?'

'What makes you say *that*?'

'Say what, Zeph?'

'About being put in the picture.'

'I only mean I'm not *with you*! You start off telling me you think something odd's going on. Then you hint it's something to do with Hugo. I'm only trying to find my bearings, old thing.'

'I'm sorry. I suppose the fact is I'm a wee bit jumpy. Where was I?'

'Something odd about Hugo. Well, what *is it*?'

'He's sunburnt.'

Margot did not say anything but her expression was eloquent.

'You don't believe me?'

'Of course I believe you, Zeph, but I must confess I don't—'

'He's got a tan on him like a life guard on Bondi Beach.'

'Well, so he's been soaking it up in a Solar Parlour. What's so odd about—'

'He hasn't. I checked.'

'Now why should you do that?'

'Because I had to be *sure*, Margot.'

The eyes of the two friends met fair and square on their respective screens. 'A U-V lamp?' suggested Margot tentatively.

'No,' said Zephyr.

'Well, he can hardly have got it from lying out on the roof. We've barely seen the sun in London for the past month.'

'Fifty-two minutes, and all but six of them during banking hours.'

'My! You *have* been busy!'

'I checked with the Met. Office.'

'You're really taking this seriously, aren't you?'

Zephyr nodded. 'I wasn't at first,' she said. 'But then I found the sand.'

'?'

'In Hugo's bed.'

'Sand in Hugo's bed,' repeated Margot feebly.

'Fine *white* sand, Margot. Coral sand!'

Margot fought down an impulse to giggle wildly. 'You had it *an*alysed?'

'I didn't need to. I recognized it at once.'

'Ah.'

'You see what I'm driving at, don't you?'

'Well, now, Zeph. Since you ask me straight out I must—'

'*Paradise Beach!*'

'Oh, Zeph! For God's *sake*!'

'I know. It's crazy.'

'But surely you've *asked* him about it? What does he—'

'Margot, how *can* I?' – it was a wail of distress – 'I mean – well, we both know it's *impossible*!'

Being a reasonably perceptive woman Margot had some inkling of why Zephyr could not simply let matters rest. However long a cable Lady Sherwood permitted herself, Sir Hugo was the Rock of Ages into which her anchor was fixed. She *had* to be sure of him, and now, for the first time in the ten years of their marriage, she was not sure: her world was shaking to its very foundations: she was finding herself in the one place she could never bear to be – outside. Admirably suppressing a desire to say: 'It serves you right, my dear', Margot nodded thoughtfully and inquired: 'Well, what now?'

Zephyr looked like a gin player whose opponent has just laid down the very card she has been waiting for. 'Would you come over for coffee tomorrow morning, Margot? About eleven?'

'To Astral Court?'

'Yes, of course.'

'All right.'

Zephyr sighed. '*Le estoy muy agradecido.*'

'*Con mucho gusto,*' replied Margot, not to be outdone.

Lady Sherwood's greeting to her friend as she opened the door of the Astral Court apartment next morning might, in more normal circumstances, have been considered somewhat eccentric. From behind her back she produced what looked like a golden-brown bootlace and proceeded to wave it before Margot's nose. 'Seaweed!' she whispered tragically. 'This morning. In the shower.'

'No land crabs yet?' inquired Margot weakly.

Zephyr shuddered. 'I haven't *dared* to look under the bed.'

They drank their coffee on the balcony overlooking Hyde Park. At Zephyr's suggestion they each had a morale-booster in the shape of a stiff peg of Napoleon 5-star cognac. Then from the pocket of her Spocorelli house-coat Zephyr produced a shiny new key which she laid on the Hester Bateman tray beside the Paul Lamarie cream-jug.

Margot peered down. 'You mean to say Hugo keeps his study locked?'

Zephyr nodded. 'Ever since I got back from Brazil.'

'Did he say why?'

'Something about *Artefax* and the re-wiring. I didn't pay much attention.'

'But, Zeph, that was over a *month* ago!'

Zephyr shrugged.

'Well, what *did* you find when you went in?'

'I haven't *been* in – yet. I only got that key cut yesterday afternoon. After I'd called you.'

'Then how do you know it fits?'

'I tried it this morning.'

'And you didn't go in?'

Zephyr shook her head. 'I just *couldn't*,' she said. 'Not on my own.'

'But this is ri*dic*ulous,' said Margot, picking up the key. 'Come on.'

She led the way purposefully up the stairs from the mezzanine, along the gallery past the bedrooms and paused outside the door of Sir Hugo's study. 'Do *you* want to?' she said. 'Or shall I?'

'You,' whispered Zephyr.

Margot put her ear to the door, held her breath, and then, somewhat absurdly, knocked. There was no response. She poked the key into the lock, twisted it firmly, turned the porcelain handle and pushed.

The door opened quite silently and the two women peered into the room. 'Well, no land crabs at any rate,' said Margot, and gave a sort of nervous hiccup of laughter.

'Look!' whispered Zephyr. 'Over there on the chair by the desk.'

'What is it?'

'His beach robe.'

Abandoning the door-knob which she had been clutching Margot advanced into the study, picked up the robe and examined it. It was faintly damp. On an impulse she raised it to her face and sniffed. It smelt rather of stale sweat. But was there something else as well? A faint, tingling aroma of iodine? Or ozone? Or salt? She dropped the garment back on to the chair and looked all round the room. 'It's darker than I remember it,' she said.

'Well, of course it is,' said Zephyr. 'He had the third window blocked up to take the anamorphic.'

As Margot padded across the deep-piled Afghan carpet to where the closed drapes concealed Igor Ketskoff's masterpiece, something crunched faintly under her foot. She stooped and thrust her fingers into the dense wool to disclose the remnants of a small crushed mollusc together with a considerable quantity of fine white sand.

'What is it?' asked Zephyr.

'Nothing,' said Margot, straightening up and twitching at the curtain. 'Where's the switch for this thing?'

'On the wall over there, I think.' Zephyr took a hesitant pace in the direction she indicated and then halted. 'You do it, Margot.'

Three steps carried Margot to the switch panel. She pushed the top button. The curtains whispered apart to reveal the 5 x 2-metre rectangle of opaque and velvet blackness. 'Ready?' she said.

Zephyr nodded dumbly.

'Here goes,' said Margot and thrust home the second button.

Even in competition with the London daylight the anamorphic still contrived to take their breath away. It was as though the mere act of throwing a switch had transported them both, miraculously and instantaneously, five thousand miles westward across the Atlantic. The sheer perfection of the illusion was utterly uncanny. And yet it was not the familiar wonder of the panorama that held them as if spellbound; rather was it the twin lines of naked footprints which strode so briskly and purposefully outward across the sand to the water's edge and then back again to the very frame of the anamorphic.

The two women, staring in numb and fascinated silence, watched the tide-nudged wavelets come lapping in like lazy tongues to lick away one print after another. Ten minutes later all that was left before their astounded gaze was the smooth silvery flank of the scoured coral and a waste of inscrutable, sparkling waters.

At that moment, with a rather harsh and unpleasant sound, Zephyr began to cry.

*

The first thing Margot did when she returned home was to try to contact Igor Ketskoff on the So-Vi. She managed it eventually and was a little piqued to realize that he had obviously forgotten who she was. Having refreshed his memory for him she saw his face take on the eager but faintly speculative expression of a cat which has heard the familiar sound of the tin-opener. 'But of *course*!' he cried. '*Chère madame Margot!* The Agatha Christie of our age! To what do I owe this pleasure?'

'It's rather awkward to explain over the So-Vi, Igor. I was wondering if you could possibly meet me for dinner this evening?'

Igor's eyebrows twitched for a calculating second and then the smile flashed on like a strip light. 'But that would be *delight*ful, madame! And where shall it be?'

'Do you know Angosturo's?'

'Indeed I do.'

'I'll book us a table right away. Would about eight suit you?'

'Admirably.'

He arrived, brimful of apologies, half an hour late, by which time Margot was already contemplating the olive at the bottom of her second martini. He snatched her hands to his lips and set about them as if they were a pair of pretzels. 'A thousand pardons, *chère madame*,' he mourned. 'I am desolated.'

'And I'm hungry,' said Margot.

'That too,' agreed Igor and clicked his fingers imperiously for the waiter. 'Another martini for madame,' he commanded. 'And for me a *pastis*.' Then he took his seat opposite her, leaned forward, and, lowering his voice, inquired meaningfully: 'And what is too awkward for you to explain to me over the So-Vi?'

'I should perhaps have said "too complicated",' replied Margot, divining that he had almost certainly misconstrued the object of her invitation.

'But Ketskoff thrives upon complexity,' said Igor smugly. 'He sucked it from his mother's teats,' adding by way of explanation: 'I am Armenian.'

Margot's eyes widened. 'An Armenian *and* a genius,' she murmured.

Igor purred. 'No doubt you are wishing to model for me?'

'Dare I?'

Igor laughed. 'Madame Margot, I like you very much. You have style. I too have style.'

'And Lady Sherwood?' inquired Margot curiously.

A shadow dusked across the dark eyes. 'No,' he said. 'Zest, yes: flamboyance, yes: style – *true* style – alas, no.' The drinks appeared and Igor raised his in a toast. 'To style,' he said.

'To style,' murmured Margot. She took a sip, smiled across at him, and decided to try the direct approach. 'Igor,' she said, 'I want to ask you a question. It may sound crazy – *I* think it *is* crazy – but even so I must hear your answer to it.'

'So? Go ahead. I like crazy questions.'

Margot took another fortifying sip at her drink. 'Would it be possible,' she said, carefully spacing out her words, 'for someone who *owned* one of your anamorphics – the person it was actually *designed* for, I mean – to—' she swallowed – 'to well – *enter* it?'

Igor looked genuinely at a loss. 'Enter it?' he echoed. 'I do not understand. You speak in metaphor, of course.'

'No. Quite literally. Could they *actually step into it*? Like you and I walked into this restaurant, say?'

Igor laughed. 'What a poetic idea! So we take a stroll through our anamorphics instead of the park! Delicious!'

'But not possible?'

'Oh, utterly impossible. An anamorphic is basically a malleable illusion – nothing more, nothing less.'

'You're quite sure of that, Igor? I mean it couldn't somehow be, well, *modified* or something?'

'Madame Margot, that I am an electronics engineer of genius I admit. Perhaps I am even something more. An artist, dare I say? But I am not, alas, a magician. Only think, for one moment, what it is you are implying by your simple question! At the very least the existence of an enantiomorphic universe and the instantaneous demolition and reconstruction of all our known scientific laws! In short, a physical impossibility. But as an *idea* – wholly enchanting!'

Margot released the breath she was not even aware she had been holding. 'And there's not the slightest chance you could be mistaken?'

'None, madame, that I do assure you. But tell me, what made you ask?'

Margot laughed. 'For a whole afternoon I've been thinking I'd hit on a simply *marvellous* way of disposing of an unwanted corpse.'

*

Aided by a capsule of *sieston*, Margot slept late. On returning from her *tête-à-tête* with Igor she had debated whether to contact Zephyr and pass on her good news, but some mildly feline streak in her character persuaded her that it could wait until the morning. After all, why should she deny Sir Hugo his little bit of fun? If anyone had earned it he had.

It was close on midday when she eventually confronted her So-Vi and tapped out the Sherwoods' code. The screen informed her that the number was temporarily unobtainable. She waited a minute, tried again, and got the same result. She was just about to look up the number of the Continental Club when she heard a buzz at her own apartment door. She walked through the minuscule hall and applied her eye to the spy-hole. 'Who is it?'

'Police.' An identity card bearing the name 'Detective Sergeant Warren' was presented to the outside lens.

Mystified, Margot slid back the safety chain and opened the door.

'Just a routine inquiry, Miss Brierly,' said the Sergeant. 'Is it all right if I come in?'

'Yes, of course.' Margot closed the door behind him and led the way into her small, book-lined sitting-room.

'I assume you've seen this morning's paper, ma'am.'

'No,' said Margot. 'Should I?'

'Ah,' said the Sergeant, 'well in that case it looks as if I've come as the bearer of some bad news.'

'What bad news?'

'Lady Sherwood is dead.'

Margot simply stared at him.

'You were a friend of hers, I believe, Miss Brierly?'

Margot nodded. 'Dead,' she repeated woodenly. 'How?'

'A fall, ma'am. Late last night.'

'What sort of a fall?'

'From the roof of Astral Court.'

'*The roof!* What in God's name was she doing up on the roof?'

'I meant from the top floor, actually. From a window. Over a hundred metres anyway.'

Margot shuddered.

The Sergeant consulted his notebook. 'I believe you called on Lady Sherwood yesterday, Miss Brierly?'

'Yes,' said Margot. 'I had coffee with her. In the morning.'

'And was she her normal self, would you say?'

'Well, yes.'

'You sound a bit hesitant.'

'Well, she *was* a bit anxious – about Sir Hugo.'

'Yes?'

'It was nothing. A sort of odd fancy she'd got. Quite absurd really.'

'And what sort of a fancy was that, Miss Brierly?'

'About an anamorphic he has – that's a kind of illusion screen – a sort of moving picture. Maybe you've seen it?'

'I think I've seen what's left of it,' said the Sergeant flatly. 'I assume that's the one.'

'In Sir Hugo's study?'

The Sergeant nodded.

'Why? What's happened to it?'

'Lady Sherwood fell through it, Miss Brierly.'

'*Through it!* Oh, but that's quite impossib—'

'Go on.'

'The window,' murmured Margot. 'It was in front of the middle window. But that window's blocked in.'

'No,' said the Sergeant. 'Just painted over black on the inside. Sir Hugo has explained to us how he didn't wish to spoil the symmetry of the façade by having it bricked up.'

'Sir Hugo was there when it happened?'

'Oh no. Lady Sherwood was alone in the apartment. Sir Hugo was officiating at a Masonic function in the City. He was actually making his speech when the accident took place.'

Margot felt as if ice-cold ants were crawling all over her body. 'Then it *was* an accident?'

'There's no question about that. As a matter of fact the only reason I'm here now is that there is one rather odd feature of the case which Sir Hugo hasn't been able to explain.'

'What was that?'

'Lady Sherwood was wearing only a bikini.'

Margot stared at him. 'Yes,' she said slowly. 'That would make sense, I suppose.'

'I don't follow you.'

'And had she been drinking too?'

'Well, officially I can't answer that till they've held the inquest. Unofficially, yes she had.'

'Dutch courage, Sergeant.'

The Sergeant's eyes went curiously opaque. 'You mean you think Lady Sherwood took her own life, Miss Brierly?'

'*Zeph! Kill herself?* Oh, good Lord, no! Not in a million years!'

'Then I'm afraid I don't—'

'You've never seen an anamorphic, have you, Sergeant? Not one that's working?'

Sergeant Warren shook his head.

'Well, you should. Because when you do you'll understand how someone who's taken on rather too much to drink *could* get it into their head that what they were seeing wasn't just an illusion but was reality itself. Providing they had the nerve to try. I believe poor Zeph was the victim of a mirage – a too-perfect illusion – and too much cognac.'

The Sergeant pursed up his lips and nodded. 'That's more or less what we thought, Miss Brierly.' He closed up his notebook and slipped it into his pocket. 'Believe me I'm sorry I had to be the one to break the news to you. You've been most helpful. I shouldn't imagine you'd be called on to give evidence at the inquest, but that's not really in my hands.'

'I understand, Sergeant. Anyway, if you do need me you know where to find me.'

Margot was not called upon. The verdict arrived at was 'Accidental Death' and the Coroner went out of his way to express the court's sympathy with the bereaved. The funeral service was private and confined to next of kin. Zephyr's body was cremated. After it was over Sir Hugo left for a holiday in the West Indies and was away for three months.

A fortnight after his return Margot was surprised to receive an invitation to dine with him one evening in Astral Court. Curiosity prompted her to accept and she arrived at the penthouse to be greeted by her sun-bronzed host who introduced her first to a ravishingly beautiful young West Indian whom she addressed as 'Blossom,' and then to Igor.

The first difference Margot noticed on entering the apartment was that the wall area on the mezzanine was once again occupied. 'A new Ketskoff?' she asked.

'Yes and no,' said Sir Hugo.

'May I see?'

'Indeed you shall, Margot. It is one of the reasons I asked you along this evening. But let us dine first. My exquisite Blossom

57

has spent all day concocting her Grenadian specialities for us, and who knows better than a Grenadian how to stimulate the jaded palate?' So saying he smiled drily and ushered them to the table.

Blossom's culinary skills fully justified Sir Hugo's advertisement. The meal was as delicious as the wines which accompanied it, and when they eventually rose from the table it was as if they were each surrounded by a private golden aura of sensual gratification.

Sir Hugo directed them to the long sofa which had been drawn round to face the curtained anamorphic and then took his place beside the control panel. 'And now, as a reward to Blossom, I intend to waft her home to Grenada.' The lights dimmed: the curtains parted. 'Olé!' cried Sir Hugo and, with an appropriate flourish, pressed the switch.

A cascade of brilliance flooded from the anamorphic like the surge of the Caribbean dawn.

Margot peered about for some sign of the repairs which Igor must have effected but there was nothing visible at all. Try as she would she simply could not visualize what must have happened. Every attempt she made to thrust Zephyr's image bodily into the panorama was frustrated by that incredible perspective. Poor Zephyr simply shrank and vanished into thin air.

As she gazed, fascinated as always by the sheer perfection of the illusion, Margot perceived, far away in the remote distance, a new movement. Shading her eyes with her hand she peered out along the curved, white sickle of the beach, under the nodding, feather-headed palms, and gradually she was able to discern the two tiny figures on horseback cantering towards her out of the distance. All along the curve of the shore they galloped, coming closer, until she could clearly make out the forms of the riders: the man, swarthy skinned, bare to the waist; the woman, wearing the briefest of bikinis, her long blonde hair streaming out along the wind to the rhythm of the ride.

They looked so happy those two, laughing as they rode; free as the sunshine and the sparkling air; the thundering hooves of their ponies – now quite distinct above the background booming of the distant surf – kicking up little shimmering fountains of rainbow spray from the edge of the sea. Right up to the anamorphic's edge they came, Zephyr and Captain Gonzales, and then they were gone, the phantom hoof-beats receding into the stereophonic distance somewhere behind Margot's head. Only the prints were left there in the sand, and the palms nodding above them in perpetual approbation.

Margot glanced sideways at Igor, wondering perhaps whether she alone had seen them, but he grinned at her cheerfully. 'Some synchro, hey?'

'*You* did it?'

'Who else? It is my latest. Are you not impressed?'

'My, I'd *love* to swim in there right now!' cried Blossom and jumping up from her place beside Margot she ran across to the wall and reached out for the beach. And, just as Margot herself once had, she drew back, frowning and rubbing her hands, complaining that it was a cheat.

Margot felt an electric tingling all up the nape of her neck. She turned back to Igor. 'When it's switched on,' she whispered, 'you *can't* touch it, can you? There's something stopping you.'

'That's right,' he said. 'The *Kappa* field.'

'So it must have been switched off when Zeph . . .'

'Of course.'

'But then there wouldn't have been any *reason* for her to—'

Igor put his lips close to her ear. 'She was blind drunk, madame. Didn't you know?'

Margot sank back into the cushions and stared, first at *Paradise Beach* and then at Sir Hugo who was now standing silhouetted before it, one arm crooked around Blossom's delectable waist, the other proudly indicating familiar features of the panorama. She thought of Zephyr, alone in this very apartment, knocking back glass after glass of brandy before making her way almost defiantly up the stairs and along the gallery. She imagined her fumbling the key into the study lock, switching on the anamorphic and staring out along that shimmering, sunlit beach. Was it then she had turned away and gone into her bedroom and changed into her costume? Or had she already done it? No, she would first have convinced herself that she hadn't been imagining it all – maybe even taking a final, reassuring look at that scrap of seaweed. Then back to the study again, her mind made up. Walking resolutely but rather unsteadily up to the wall. Taking a chair to climb on, wobbling a bit, leaning forward, pressing with her palms flat against that unyielding field, till in the end all her weight was straining forward . . . But even so she *still* couldn't have reached the switch herself. Someone else *must* have done it. Someone actually *there*, in the room with her. And there had been no one. The inquest had confirmed it. No one at all.

'Coffee, madam? Black or white?'

Deferential as ever, programmed to perfection, the auto-butler was standing at her elbow, proffering his tray. Strong, slender metal fingers hovered above the cream jug. So unobtrusive. So discreet. A paragon among servants.

'Black, please,' said Margot faintly.

Piper at the Gates of Dawn

Among the twenty-two books which comprise the Avian
Apocrypha, the one which has been called by certain scholars
'Old Peter's Tale' and by others 'The Book of Gyre' has
always occupied a place somewhat apart from the rest.

Recent close textual and stylistic analysis by Professor J. P.
Hollins and others would appear to have confirmed the
presence of no fewer than three distinct contributing hands, at
least two of which have been confidently identified with the
anonymous authors of 'The Book of Morfedd' and 'Orgen's
Dream'.

In electing to offer to a wider public this new version
compiled from the three earliest extant manuscripts I have
purposely eschewed the two titles by which the work is
generally familiar and have chosen instead that under which
the story appears in the 'Carlisle m.s.' (circa AD 3300).

R.J.C. St Malcom's College Oxford June 3798

Cold curtains of November rain came drifting slowly up the
valley like an endless procession of phantom mourners following
an invisible hearse. From beneath an overhang of limestone a boy
and an old man squatted side by side and gazed disconsolately
out across the river to the dripping forest on the far bank.
Suddenly a salmon leapt – a flicker of silver in the gloom and a
splash like a falling log. The boy's eyes gleamed. 'Ah,' he
breathed. 'Did you see him?'

The old man grunted.

'I'm going to try for him, Peter.'

The man glanced round out of the tail of his eyes and sniffed
sceptically. 'What with?'

The boy unfastened the thong of his leather knapsack, delved
inside, and pulled out a slender double-barrelled wooden pipe –

61

something between a twin-stemmed whistle and a recorder. He rubbed it briskly on the sleeve of his grey woollen pullover then set the mouthpiece to his lips and blew softly. A note, clear and liquid as a blackbird's, floated out from beneath his fingers. Another followed, and another, and then came a little frisking trill that set the old man's pulse fluttering.

'Who taught you to play like that, lad?'

'Morfedd.'

The boy rose to his feet, stepped out into the rain, and had taken four or five paces down the slope towards the river's edge when the old man called him back. 'Here,' he said, pulling off his cap and flinging it across. 'It'll keep the rain off your neck.'

The boy grinned his thanks, dragged the waxed leather scuttle over his untidy mop of black curls, and skipped down to where a flat rock jutted out into the stream. There he squatted, as close as he could get to the hurrying tawny water, and once more put the pipe to his lips.

Squinting through the veiling rain, the old man became uncomfortably aware of a chill area around the back of his neck where his cap had been and he hunched down deeper into the collar of his sheepskin coat. Like wisps of gossamer, odd disconnected threads of music came floating up to him from the rain-pocked waters below and, as he half-listened, there suddenly flickered unbidden across his mind's eye a lightning-sharp vision of a large and succulent dragonfly. So vivid was the image that for a confusing second he was convinced the insect was hovering a mere handspan before his nose. Next instant there was an excited shouting from below, a flurry of splashing, and he saw the boy staggering among the rain-wet boulders at the water's edge with a huge silver fish struggling in his arms.

With an alacrity which wholly belied his years the old man scrambled down the bank just in time to prevent the boy from measuring his own length in a pool. He grabbed at the gulping salmon, thrust his thumbs firmly into its gills and contrived to bang its head against a rock. 'Blast me, boy!' he cried. 'I never saw such luck in all my days! Blast me if I did!'

The boy laughed delightedly. 'He's *big*, isn't he? Did you see him jump? Right up at me! *Swoosh!*'

The old man lifted the shuddering fish and contrived to hold it out at arm's length. 'I'll swear he's nigh on ten kils,' he panted. 'A regular whale! What are we going to do with him?'

'Why, eat him, of course.'

'Ah, some for sure, lad. The rest we'd best try to smoke. But we've got to get ourselves across the stream first. With all this rain, by nightfall she'll be up to twice your own height, and it's ten lom or more round by Kirkby bridge. Nip you up aloft and fetch the packs. We'll try for a crossing up around the bend.'

The boy clambered back up to the overhang and ducked out of sight. The old man selected a stout stick from among a tangle of driftwood, took a clasp knife from his pocket and, having sharpened one end of the stick to a point, spiked it through the salmon's gills and hefted the fish up on to his back.

Twenty minutes later the two of them were over the river and picking their way along the deer track that followed the far bank. By then the rain had eased off to a steady, depressing drizzle. Though it was barely two hours gone noon, the low clouds and the brooding forest dimmed the light almost to curfew gloom. Conversation between the two travellers was restricted to grunts of warning and acknowledgement as the old man negotiated rocks and exposed tree roots which had been made even more treacherous by the rain.

They had covered some two kilometres in this fashion when the track broadened out perceptibly into a discernible path. The boy at once seized the opportunity to move up to the old man's side. 'Will we reach Sedbergh before nightfall, Peter?'

'Not without breaking our necks, we won't. But I recall a 'stead hereabouts might lodge us for the night. I've been trying to bring the man's given name to mind, but it's twenty year or more since I last trod this track.'

'A farmer, is he?'

'Bit of everything as I recall it. Like most of 'em round here. Newton? Norton? *Norris! That's* the name! Norris Cooperson! Yes, yes, now it comes back. Old Sam Cooperson was a colour-sergeant in Northumberland's dragoons. Won his freedom in the Battle of Rotherham in '950. That takes us back a bit, doesn't it? Old Sam leased a stretch of the Lord's grazing down the river a way. Did well enough for his boy to buy the freehold. I seem to recall that young Norris wed a lass from Aysgarth. And didn't her people have property round York? Or was it Scarborough? Funny how his name slipped me. Norris. Norris Cooperson. Aye, that's him.'

'Where does he live, Peter?'

'On a bit yet. I seem to mind a beck slipping down from the fells. Old Sam built his 'stead facing south-west, backing right up into the hills. "Guarding his rear" he called it.' The old man chuckled. 'Sergeant Cooperson had had a Jock spear up his arse in his time, so he knew what he was talking about.'

They came to a waist-high wall of rough stone which had recently been repaired, clambered over it, and headed off on a diagonal course away from the river. After they had gone about five hundred paces the old man paused, lifted his head, and snuffed the air like a dog. The boy watched him closely. 'Smoke?' he asked.

'Horses,' said the old man. 'Smoke too. It can't be far now.'

The ground rose slightly and the forest trees began to thin out almost as if they were withdrawing fastidiously from a contact which was distasteful to them. The two wayfarers trudged up to the crest of the rise and saw below them and a long bowshot off to their left, the low outline of a substantial stone stable, a bracken-thatched barn, a farm house and a scattering of timber outbuildings. A herd of long-horned, hump-backed cattle was grazing in the meadow which sloped gently down from the homestead to the distant river.

The old man shifted the salmon from one shoulder to the other and nodded with satisfaction. 'I wasn't wrong, was I, Tom? But it's grown a fair bit since I last set eye on it. Reckon you'd best get yourself a stick while you can. They're bound to have a dog or two.'

The boy shook his head. 'They won't bother me.'

'It's not *you* I'm feared for, lad. It's our supper here.'

The boy unfastened his knapsack and again took out his pipe. 'Dogs are the easiest of all,' he said scornfully. 'They'll believe *anything*.'

The old man studied him thoughtfully, sucked a tooth, seemed on the point of saying something and then, apparently, changed his mind. Side by side they plodded off down the hill towards the farm.

The shaggy cattle raised their heads at their approach, regarded them with mild, munching curiosity and then nodded back to their grazing. They had passed almost through the herd before the farm dogs got wind of them. They came hurtling out from behind the stables, three lean, vicious-looking fell hounds, snarling and yelping in their eagerness to savage the intruders.

The boy stood his ground; calmly waited till the leader was but a short stone's throw distant; then set the pipe to his lips and blew a series of darting notes of so high a pitch that the old man's ears barely caught them. But the dogs did. They stopped almost dead in their tracks, for all the world as if they had run full tilt into a solid wall of glass. Next moment the three of them were lying stretched out full length on the wet grass, whining, with their muzzles clasped in their forepaws and their eyes closed.

The boy played a few more notes then walked forward and prodded the largest of the curs with his toe. The animal rolled over on to its back and offered its unguarded throat to him in a drooling ecstasy of abject submission. 'You see,' said the boy disdainfully. 'They're such ninnies they'll even believe they're puppies.'

The barking had brought a woman to the door of the farm house and now she called out to the dogs. Slowly, dazedly, they rose to their feet, shook themselves and loped off towards her, pausing every so often to glance back and whimper perplexedly.

'And who might you be, strangers?'

With his spare hand the old man doffed his cap, allowing the damp breeze to flutter his white hair. 'Old Peter the Tale-Spinner of Hereford, Ma'am. Legging for York City. This here's young Tom, my niece's lad. We missed our way short-cutting it through Haw Gill. We'd be glad to pay silver for a night's dry lodging.'

'My goodman's out timbering,' responded the woman doubt-fully. 'I dursent say you yea or nay without he's back.'

'That would be goodman Norris, I dare say, ma'am?'

'Aye,' she said, screwing up her eyes to see him better. 'Aye, it would.'

'Then you must be Mistress Cooperson.'

'Aye,' she admitted. 'What of it?'

'Tell me, mistress, does Old Sam's halberd still hang bright over the chimney-breast?'

The woman raised her right hand in a strange, hesitant little half-gesture of uncertainty. 'You'll have been here afore then, old man?'

'Aye, ma'am. Close on twenty year since. Just agin you and young Norris wed, that would a' been.' He cocked an eye up at the sagging, dripping clouds. 'If me 'n the lad could maybe

65

step inside your barn yonder, we'd hold it more than kind. This wet strikes a deathly chill into old bones.'

The woman flushed. 'No, no,' she said, backing over the threshold. 'Come you in here and dry yourselves by the fire. It's just me and the young lass alone, you see.' Then, by way of explanation, she added: 'We heard tell there was an Irish raider into Morecambe Bay afore Holymass.'

'That's real kind in you, ma'am.' The old man beamed, swinging the salmon down off his back and holding it out towards her. 'We even thought to bring some supper with us, you see.'

'Oh, there's a wild beauty!' she exclaimed. 'How came you by him?'

'Singing for our supper, you might say,' said the old man winking at the boy. 'I've been thinking we could maybe split master silversides longwise and perhaps smoke one half of him in your chimney overnight. That way you'll have a fine supper and we'll have ourselves fare for our morrow's footing.'

'Yes, yes,' she said. 'There's oak afire this minute. Do you bring him through here into the scullery.' She called round over her shoulder: 'Katie, lass! Come and liven up that fire right sharp!'

A blue-eyed girl of about twelve, with hair so palely blonde it was almost white, emerged from the shadows, took a long hard stare at the visitors and then vanished. The old man wiped the mud from his boots on the bundle of dried bracken piled for the purpose just inside the doorway, then carted the salmon through into the scullery and flopped it out on the slab of dark green slate which the woman indicated. She reached down a knife and a steel from a shelf and honed a rapid edge. Then with the skill of long practice she slit the fish down the belly and began scooping its insides into a wooden bucket.

The boy meanwhile had wandered through into the long stone-flagged kitchen and now stood silently watching the girl arranging dry oak billets against the smouldering back-log in the huge fireplace. She glanced at him over her shoulder. 'You can blow, can't you, boy?'

He nodded, moved across and knelt beside her as she crushed dry bracken up into a ball and thrust it into the space behind the propped logs. 'Well, go on then,' she commanded. 'Show me.'

Obediently the boy leant forward and puffed till the white

ashes leapt aside and exposed the glowing embers beneath. He reached out, pressed the bracken down and blew again. The kindling began to smoke. Next moment a tiny snakestongue of flame had flickered up. He blew more gently, fanning the flame till the whole ball was well ablaze and then he sat back on his heels and brushed the powder of ash from his cheeks and eyebrows.

The girl laid a few sticks across the flames and turned to him again. 'What're you going to York for?'

'To Chapter School.'

'What's that?'

'My cousin's spoken me a place in the Minster choir. He's Clerk to the Chapter.'

'What'll you do?'

'Learn to read and write. Sing in the choir. Maybe play too.'

'Play what? Your pipe?'

He nodded.

She studied him long and hard by the light of the spurtling flames. 'I saw what you did to the dogs,' she said thoughtfully.

He smiled. 'Oh, that was easy. The fish was much harder.'

'You did that to the fish too? What you did to the dogs?'

'Sort of,' he said.

'How do you do it?'

His smile broadened but he said nothing.

'Can I see your pipe?'

'All right.' He got up, walked over to the doorway where he had left his pack, took out the pipe and brought it back to her. She held it in both hands and examined it by the firelight. Deep inside one of the tubes some crystalline facet caught the flames and twinkled like a diamond. She raised the mouthpiece to her lips and was just about to blow when he snatched the instrument from her. 'No,' he said. 'No, you mustn't. It's tuned to me, you see.'

'That's daft,' she said, her cheeks flushing scarlet. 'How could I hurt the silly thing?'

'I'm sorry, Katie. I can't explain it to you.' He stroked his fingers in a slow caress all down the length of the pipe and then looked up at her. 'You see, Morfedd made it for *me*.'

'Morfedd? The Wizard of Bowness?'

'Yes.'

'You *knew* him?'

The boy nodded. 'Morfedd's in here,' he said, lifting the pipe. 'And in me.'

'Who says so?'

'It's true, Katie. He chose me on my third birthnight – ten summers ago. He twinned my tongue for me. Look.' His lips parted and the tip of a pink tongue slipped out between the white, even teeth. As Katie watched, fascinated, the boy's tongue-tip divided and the two halves flickered separately up and down before flicking back into his mouth. 'Believe me now?' he asked and grinned at her.

The girl's blue eyes were very wide indeed. 'Did it hurt?' she whispered.

'No, not much. He did it bit by bit.' The boy held up the pipe and pointed to the twin air ducts. 'You see he wanted me to be able to tongue them both separately,' he said. 'Listen.'

He set the pipe to his lips and blew gently down it. Then, without moving his fingers, he sounded two gentle trills, one slow, one faster; yet both somehow intertwined and as sweetly melodious as two birds warbling in unison in a green glade of the deep forest.

Katie was utterly enraptured. She had quite forgiven him his ill-mannered snatching of the pipe. 'Play me a tune, Tom,' she begged. 'Go on. Do. Please.'

'All right,' he agreed. 'What would you like?'

'I don't know. Make one up. Just for me. Could you?'

Tom rubbed his nose with the back of his hand then he turned slowly to face her and gazed deep into her eyes. As he did so he seemed to go very, very still, almost as if he were listening to some sound which only he could hear. For perhaps a minute he sat thus, then he nodded once, set the pipes to his lips and began to play.

Norris and his two grown-up sons returned from the forest at dusk. Well before the others heard them Tom's sharp ears had picked up the distant jingle of traces and the squeal of wooden axles. A moment later the dogs gave tongue to a raucous chorus of welcome. Katie and her mother hustled round making the final preparations for supper while Tom and old Peter sat one on either side of the fire, steaming faintly in the drowsy warmth.

Norris was the first to enter. A thickset, heavily bearded man, with greying hair and eyes the colour of an April sky. He dragged off his hooded leather tippet and slung it up on to an iron hook. almost at once it began to drip quietly on to the flagstones beneath. 'Halloa, there!' he cried. 'What's this then? Company?'

Old Peter and Tom had risen at his entry and now the old man called out: 'You'll remember me, I think, Norris? Peter the Tale-Spinner. Son of Blind Hereford.'

'Sweet God in Heaven!' exclaimed Norris striding to meet him. 'Not the Prince of Liars in person? Aye, it's him, right enough! Welcome back, old rogue! I'd given you over for worms' meat years ago!'

They clasped forearms in the pool of yellow lamp-light and shook their heads over one another. 'And who's the sprig, then?' demanded Norris tipping his chin at Tom. 'One of yours?'

'My niece Margot's lad. Tom by given name. Margot wed with a Stavely man. I'm taking the boy to York for her.'

'York, eh? And legging it? Ah so, you shall tell us all over supper. Well met, old man. What's ours is yours. And you too, boy. Katie, wench! Is my water hot?'

He strode off towards the scullery, boisterous as the North wind, and soon they heard sounds of noisy blowing and sluicing as he swilled himself down at the stone sink. His wife came into the kitchen and clattered out wooden bowls and mugs down the long table. 'He remembered you then?' she said with a smile.

'Aye,' said Peter. 'I've changed less than he has, it seems. Not that he hasn't worn well, mind you.' He tipped his head to one side. 'How comes your lass by that barley mow of hers?'

'Bar me all my folks are fair,' she said. 'Katie's eyes are her Dad's though. The boys seemed to fall betwixt and between.' She stepped up to the fireplace, caught up a corner of her apron and lifted the lid of the iron cauldron which hung from a smoke-blackened chain above the flames. A rich and spicy scent floated over the hearth. She nodded, re-settled the lid and squinted up into the chimney where the other half of the salmon could be dimly seen twisting slowly back and forth in the hot air and the blue-grey woodsmoke. 'Let it down again, lad,' she said. 'We'll souse it just once more.'

Tom unhooked an end of the chain and lowered the fish till she was able to reach it. 'Hold it still now,' she said and picking a brush of twigs out of a pot on the hearth she basted the now golden flesh till it gleamed like dark honey. 'Up with it, lad.'

The fish vanished once more up the throat of the flue and a

few aromatic drops fell down and sizzled among the embers.

As Tom was making the chain fast the door to the yard opened and Norris' two sons came in followed by the three dogs. The men eyed the two strangers curiously and watched without speaking as the dogs bounded up to the hearth and then ranged themselves in a grinning, hopeful semi-circle round the boy who looked down at them and laughed.

Norris appeared at the scullery door towelling his neck and bawled out introductions as though he were calling cattle in from the fells. The young men nodded and flashed their teeth in smiles of welcome. 'You must have got a way with dogs, lad,' observed one. 'That lot don't take kindly to strangers as a rule. They're like as not to have the arse out of your breeks.'

Tom eyed the dogs and shook his head. Then Katie came in and summoned them to her. In her hand she held the wooden bucket of fish offal. She opened the yard door, stepped outside, and the dogs tumbled after her, whining eagerly.

Ten minutes later the men and the boy took their places at the long table. Katie's mother ladled out thick broth into wooden bowls and Katie set one before each guest, then one before her father and her brothers and, last of all, one each for her mother and herself. Norris dunked his spoon and sucked up a noisy mouthful. 'My women tell me we've got you to thank for this,' he said to Peter.

The old man shrugged modestly and winked across at Tom. 'You wed a fine cook, Norris,' he said. 'I've not tasted such a broth since I sampled your mother's.'

Norris smiled. 'Aye, old Mam taught Annie a thing or two afore she went. How to bear strong men for a start. Now tell us some news, old timer. Is it true there's a new king in Wales?'

'Aye. Dyfydd men call him. They say he's a fierce and cunning fighter.'

'That's as may be, but can he keep the peace? Hold off the Paddys? Hey?'

'Maybe. Along the west border there was talk of him laying court to Eileen of Belfast – King Kerrigan's widow. That might do it – if he pulls it off.'

'The sooner the better,' said Norris, reaching out and tearing a ragged lump from the wheaten loaf before him. 'You heard they'd fired Lancaster Castle?'

'There's no truth in that story, Norris. They were held at Morecambe and hanged at Preston.'

'Is that a fact?'

'I did a two-day telling in Lancaster myself a month back. On my way up to Kendal. By the time we leg it into York I dare say folk will be telling us the Paddys hold everything west of the Pennines.'

Norris laughed. 'Aye. If cows grew like rumours we'd none of us lack for beef.'

Peter smiled and nodded. 'Are you still under Northumberland's shield here?'

'For what it's worth. The last border patrol we saw was nigh on a year back, and they were a right bunch of thieves. No, the only time his Lordship wants to know about us is at the Mid-Summer Tax Harvest. Our trouble here is that there aren't enough of us freeholders to make up more than a token force. And we're spread too thin. The Paddys could pick us off one by one if they'd a mind to, and none of the rest of us would be a wit the wiser till it was too late. It's our luck there's not much up here they're likely to fancy.'

'You've not been troubled then?'

'Nothing to speak of.'

The younger son glanced round at his brother and murmured something too low for Peter to catch.

'Poachers?' Peter asked.

'We had a spot of bother a year or two back. That's all settled now. Let's have some more beer here, Katie, lass!'

The girl brought a huge stone jug and refilled her father's mug. 'Dad *killed* one of them,' she said to Peter. 'With his axe. You did, didn't you, Dad?'

'It was them or us,' said Norris. 'Don't think I'm proud of it.'

'Well, *I* am,' said Katie stoutly.

Norris laughed and gave her a cheerful wallop on the behind. 'Well, it seems to have taught them a lesson,' he said. 'We've not been troubled since. Now tell us how the world's been treating you, Tale-Spinner.'

'Never better than this,' said Peter taking a long pull at his beer. 'I crossed the narrow seas; lived a while in France and Italy. Joined up with a Greek juggler and voyaged with him to the Americas. Made some money and lost it. Came home to die

71

two years ago. That's about it, Norris. Nothing you've any call to envy me for.'

'You've never felt you wanted to settle then?'

'It's not so much a question of *wanting*, Norris; more a question of *royals*. Some can save money; some can't. Mind you, I'll not say I haven't had my chances. I was three whole years in one town in Italy. Still got connections there in a manner of speaking. But I'll not be putting to sea again. These bones will lie in the Fifth Kingdom. All I'm waiting for now is to see the millennium out.'

Katie's mother spooned out steaming portions of rosy fish on to the wooden platters, piled potatoes and onions around them and passed them down the table. Norris stretched out and helped himself liberally to salt. 'And just what's so special about the year 3000?' he demanded. 'A year's a year and that's all there is to it. Numbers aren't worth a pig's turd.'

'Ah, now, if you'll pardon me for saying so, Norris, there you're mistaken. The fact is the world's grown to expect something remarkable of AD 3000. And if enough people get to expecting something, then like enough it'll come to pass.'

'Peace and Brotherhood, you mean? The White Bird of Kinship and all that froth? I just wish someone would have a go at telling it to the Paddys and the Jocks.'

'Ah, but they believe in it too, Norris.'

'Oh, they do, do they?' Norris snorted. 'It's the first I've heard of it. If you ask me the only time the Jocks and the Paddys are likely to fall on anyone's neck is when they've got a broadsword to hand.'

'There'll be a sign,' said Peter. 'That's how it'll be.'

'A sign, eh? What sort of sign?'

'Some speak of a comet or a silver sky ship like they had in the Old Times. In Italy there was talk of a new star so bright you'll be able to see it in the day sky.'

'And what do you think?'

'Well, they could be right, Norris. Stranger things have happened.'

'No doubt. And telling people about them has kept your old belly nicely lined, eh?'

'Someone has to do it.'

'Oh, I'm not belittling you, old timer. In truth I sometimes think we need more like you. Faith, it's a poor lookout for folks if they can see no more to life than scratching for food and working up their appetite for it by killing their fellow men.' He waved his knife at Tom. 'What do you say, boy?'

Tom swallowed his mouthful and nodded his head. 'Yes, sir,' he said. 'There *is* more than that.'

'Bravely said, lad! Well, go on, tell us about it.'

'Peter's right, sir. About the White Bird, I mean. It *is* coming.'

'Oh, yes?' said Norris, winking at Peter. 'What'll it be like, son?'

'I mean for some of us it's here *already*, sir,' said Tom. 'We can hear it *now*. It's in everything – all about us – everywhere. That's what I thought you meant, sir.'

Norris blinked at him and rolled his tongue pensively around his teeth. Then he nodded his head slowly. 'Well now, maybe I did at that,' he said. 'Not that I'd have thought to put it just so myself.'

'Tom's a piper, Dad,' said Katie. 'He plays better than anyone I've ever heard.'

'Is that a fact?' said Norris. 'Then after supper we'll have to see if we can't persuade him to give us a tune. How about it, lad?'

'Gladly, sir,'

'Good,' said Norris stabbing a fork into his food and turning back to Peter. 'You use him in your tellings, do you?'

'Not so far,' said the old man. 'But the thought crossed my mind just this afternoon. There's no denying he's got a real gift for the pipes. What do you say, Tom, lad? Fancy coming into partnership?'

'I thought you were supposed to be taking him to the Chapter School at York,' said Katie's mother with an edge to her voice that was not lost on Peter.

'Why, to be sure I am, ma'am,' he said. 'We're legging by way of Sedbergh and Aysgarth. Aiming to strike York for Christmas. That's so, isn't it, Tom?'

The boy nodded.

'I was hoping to make a start two weeks ago but I got an invitation to a telling in Carlisle which held me back.' The old man cocked a ragged eyebrow towards Katie's mother. 'I seem to recall you to be a native of Aysgarth, ma'am.'

'You've got a fine memory, Tale-Spinner.'

'I was thinking that maybe you would like us to carry some message to your folks for you?'

'You'd have to leg a deal further than Aysgarth to do it, old man,' she said and smiled wanly. 'They're dead and gone long since.'

'Is that so? Well, indeed I'm truly sorry to hear it.'

'It happens,' she said.

Supper over, Norris tapped a small cask of strong ale, drew it off into a substantial earthenware jug, added sliced apple and a fragrant lump of crushed honeycomb, then stood the mixture down on the hearth to mull. By the time Tom had finished helping Katie and her mother to clear the table and wash the dishes, the warm ale was giving off a drowsy scent which set an idle mind wandering dreamily down the long-forgotten hedge-rows of distant summers.

They settled themselves in a semicircle round the hearth; the lamp was trimmed and turned low, and old Peter set about earning his night's lodging. Having fortified himself with a draught of ale, he launched himself into a saga set in the days before the Drowning when the broad skies were a universal highway and, by means of strange skills, long since forgotten, men and women could sit snug and cosy by their own firesides and see in their magic mirrors things which were happening at that very instant on the other side of the world.

Like all good stories there was some love in it and much adventure; hardship, breath-taking coincidence and bloody slaughter; and finally, of course, a happy ending. Its hero, the young Prince Amulet, having discovered that his noble father the King of Denmark has been murdered by a wicked brother who has usurped the throne, sets out to avenge the crime. Peter's description of the epic duel fought out between uncle and nephew with swords whose blades were beams of lethal light, held Norris and his family open-mouthed and utterly spell-bound. Not for nothing was the son of Blind Hereford known throughout the Seven Kingdoms as 'the Golden-Tongued'.

When the victorious Prince and his faithful Princess had finally been escorted to their nuptial chamber through a fanfare of silver trumpets the enchanted listeners broke into spontaneous applause and begged Peter for another. But the Tale-Spinner was too old and wise a bird to be caught so easily. Pleading that his throat was bone dry he reminded them that young Tom had agreed to favour them with a tune or two.

'Aye, come along, lad,' said Norris. 'Let's have a taste of that whistle of yours.'

While Tom was fetching his instrument from his pack, Katie made a round of the circle and replenished the mugs. Then she settled herself at her father's knee. The boy sat down cross-legged on the fire-warmed flagstones and waited till everyone was still.

He had played scarcely a dozen notes when there was a sound of frantic scratching at the yard door and a chorus of heart-rending whimpers. Tom broke off and grinned up at Norris. 'Shall I let them in?'

'I will,' said Katie and was up and away before Norris had a chance to say either yes or no.

The dogs bounded into the kitchen, tails waving ecstatically, and headed straight for the boy. He blew three swift, lark-high notes, pointed to the hearth before him and meek as mice they stretched themselves out at his feet. He laughed, leant forward and tapped each animal on its nose with his pipe. 'Now you behave yourselves, dogs,' he said, 'or I'll scare your tails off.'

Katie regained her place and he began to play once more. He had chosen a set of familiar country dances and, within seconds, he had feet tapping and hands clapping all around the circle. It was almost as if the listeners were unable to prevent their muscles from responding to the imperious summons of his jigs and reels. Even Old Peter found his toes twitching and his fingers drumming out the rhythms on the wooden arm of the ingle-nook settle.

With the flamelight flickering elvishly in his grey-green eyes Tom swung them from tune to tune with an effortless dexterity that would surely have been the envy of any professional four times his age, and when he ended with a sustained trill which would not have shamed a courting blackbird his audience showered praise upon him.

'Blest if ever I heard better piping!' cried Norris. 'Who taught you such skills, lad?'

'Morfedd the Wizard did,' said Katie. 'That's right, isn't it, Tom?'

Tom nodded, staring ahead of him into the flames.

'Morfedd of Bowness, eh?' said Norris. 'Me, I never met him. But I recall how in Kendal the folk used to whisper that he'd

75

stored up a treasurehouse of wisdom from the Old Times and Lord knows what else beside. How came he to teach you piping, lad?'

'He came for me on my third birthnight,' said Tom. 'He'd heard me playing a whistle up on the fells and he bespoke my Mum and Dad for me.' He raised his head and looked round at Norris. 'After Morfedd died,' he said, 'I composed a lament for him. Would you like to hear it?'

'Aye, lad. That we would. Whenever you're ready.'

Then Tom did a strange thing. He gripped the pipe in both hands, one at either end, and held it out at arm's length in front of him. Then, very slowly, he brought it back towards his chest, bent his head over it and seemed to be murmuring something to it. It was a strangely private little ritual of dedication that made all those who saw it wonder just what kind of a child this was. Next moment he had set the pipe to his lips, closed his eyes and turned his soul adrift.

To their dying day none of those present ever forgot the next ten minutes and yet no two of them ever recalled it alike. But all were agreed on one thing. The boy had somehow contrived to take each of them, as it were, by the hand and lead them back to some private moment of great sadness in their own lives, so that they felt again, deep in their own hearts, all the anguish of an intense but long-forgotten grief. For most the memory was of the death of someone dearly loved, but for young Katie it was different and was somehow linked with some exquisite quality she sensed within the boy himself – something which carried with it an almost unbearable sense of terrible loss. Slowly it grew within her, swelling and swelling till in the end, unable to contain it any longer she burst into wild sobs and buried her face in her father's lap.

Tom's fingers faltered on the stops and those listening who were still capable of doing so, noticed that his own cheeks were wet with tears. He drew in a great, slow, shuddering breath, then, without saying a word, got up and walked away into the shadows by the door. One by one the dogs rose to their feet and padded after him. Having restored his pipe to its place within his pack he opened the door and stepped outside into the night.

It was a long time before anyone spoke and, when they did, what was said was oddly inconsequential: Norris repeating dully, 'Well, I dunno, I dunno, I dunno,' and Old Peter muttering

what sounded like a snatch from one of his own stories – 'And
the angel of Grief moved invisible among them and their tears
fell like summer rain.' Only Katie's mother was moved to
remark: 'He'll not carry such a burden for long, I think,' though
had anyone thought to ask her, she would have been hard put to
explain what she meant, or even why she had said it.

During the night the wind shifted into a new quarter. It came
whistling down, keen and chill from the Northern Cheviots,
until the dawn sky, purged at last of cloud, soared ice-blue and
fathomless above the forest and the fells.

A bare half-hour after sun-up Old Peter and Tom had said
their farewells and were on their way. Katie accompanied them
to the top of the valley to set them on their path. She pointed to
a white rock on the crest of a distant hill and told them that from
there they would be able to sight Sedbergh spire. The old man
thanked her and said he'd be sure to call and see her again when
he was next in the district.

'You may be,' she said, 'but he won't. I know,' and turning
to Tom she took from the pocket of her cloak a small, flat, green
pebble, washed smooth by the river. A hole had been drilled in
the centre and through it a leather lace was threaded. 'That's for
my song,' she said. 'Keep it. It may bring you luck.'

Tom nodded, slid the thong over his head and slipped the
talisman down inside his jerkin where it lay cool as a water drop
against his chest. 'Good-bye, Katie,' he said.

He did not look back until they were well down the track and
then he saw her still standing there on the hilltop with the wind
streaming out her long hair into a misty golden halo. He raised
his arm in salute. She waved back, briefly, and the next moment
she had turned and vanished in the direction of the hidden farm.

They stopped to eat shortly before noon, choosing the shelter
of an outcrop of rock close to where a spring bubbled. The sun
struck warm on to their backs even though, but a few paces from
where they sat, the wind still hissed drearily through the dry
bracken bones. Old Peter broke in two the flat scone which
Katie's mother had given them and then divided one of the
halves into quarters. He sliced off two substantial lumps of the
smoked salmon and handed bread and meat to the boy.

For a few minutes they both chewed away in silence then
Peter said: 'I'd been thinking of trying our luck at Sedbergh

Manor, but maybe we'd do better at the inn. There's a chance we'll strike up acquaintance with a carrier and get ourselves a lift to Aysgarth. Better ride than leg, eh?'

'Whatever you say,' agreed Tom.

The old man nodded sagely. 'If luck's with us there's no reason we shouldn't pick up a royal or two into the bargain. Between the two of us, I mean. Reckon we could milk it out of them, eh?'

Tom glanced across at him but said nothing.

'You've never thought of roading for a living then, lad?'

'No.'

'Ah, it's the only life if you've got the talent for it. Blast, but we two'd make a splendid team! Think of legging the high road through the Seven Kingdoms! York, Derby, Norwich, London. New towns, new faces! Why, we could even duck it across the French seas an' we'd a mind to! Taste the salt spray on our lips and see the silver sails swell like a sweetheart's bosom! How's that strike you as fare for a spring morning, lad?'

Tom smiled. 'But I thought you said you weren't going to go to sea again.'

'Ah, well, that was just a *façon de parler* as they say across the water. But with you along it would be different. We could work up a proper act, see? You'd feel your way into the mood of each tale and then, with that pipe of yours, you'd come drifting in along o' the words like a feather on the tide. Between the two of us we'd reach right down through their ears and tickle their pockets. Blast it, Tom lad, I tell you you've got a touch of magic in those finger-ends of yours – a gift like nobody's business! You don't want to chuck all that away while you choke yourself to death on Minster dust! A dower like yours cries out to be shared! You owe it to the Giver of Gifts! Out there on the wide high road you'll be as free as the wind and the birds of the air! Up and off! Over the hills and far away!'

Tom laughed. 'But I *am* free. Morfedd taught me that. He unlocked something inside me and let it fly out. Besides, I want to learn how to read and write.'

'Pooh, there's nothing to letters, Tom. I'll teach you myself. And more besides! There's only one school for the likes of us, lad. The great high road. Once you've begun to turn the pages of that book you'll never want another.'

'And Mum? What would she think? After she's taken all that trouble to bespeak Cousin Seymour for me?'

'Ah, your heart does you credit, lad. Real credit. But I know my Mistress Margot. Been dreaming up plans for you, hasn't she? How maybe you'll catch the Bishop's eye and gain a preference and so on and so forth? Isn't that it? Ah, that's just a mother's daydreams, Tom. Believe you me, lad, the only way to preference in York Chapter for a boy like you is up the back stairs and on to the choirmaster's pallet. Faith, I tried to tell her so, but she wouldn't listen. Said your Cousin Seymour would shield you from anything of that sort. But I know the ways of the world and—'

'People become what you think them, Peter.'

'Eh? How's that?'

'Morfedd said so. He said our thoughts are unseen hands shaping the people we meet. Whatever we truly think them to be, that's what they'll become for us.'

The old man stared at him, wondering if the Kendal gossips had spoken true and the boy really *was* touched. 'Oh, he did, did he?' he said at last. 'And what else did he say?'

'Morfedd? Oh, lots of things.'

'Well, go on, lad. Let's hear one.'

Tom rubbed his nose with the back of his hand and stared out across the hillside. 'He used to say that seeing things as they *really* are is the most difficult seeing of all. He said people only see what they want to see. And then they believe the truth is what they *think* they see, not what really is.'

'Aye, well, I'm not saying he doesn't have a point there. But I'll warrant he didn't think to tell you how to recognize this truth when you do see it.'

'You don't *see* it exactly. You *feel* it.'

'And just how's that supposed to help someone like me who lives by his lying? Didn't you know they call me "Prince of Liars"?'

Tom grinned. 'Oh, that's different,' he said. 'Your stories are like my music. They tell a different kind of truth. People hear it in their hearts.'

'Blast it, boy, you have an answer pat for everything! Look here, I'll tell you what. From now till Christmastide we'll work the road 'twixt here and York – Leyburn, Masham, Ripon and Boroughbridge – finishing up at The Duke's Arms in Selby

Street. That way you'll get a fair taste of the life I'm offering. Then if you're still set on the Chapter School, why that's all there is to it. Till then you'll have a third-part share in all we take. That strike you as fair?'

'All right,' said Tom. 'But you must tell me what you want me to do.'

'Done!' cried Peter. 'We'll set it up while we're legging down to Sedbergh. Have you done with eating? Right then, partner, let's be on our way.'

It soon emerged that the book of the open road which Peter had recommended to Tom with such enthusiasm contained at least one chapter which he himself had never read. By the third week of December when they reached Boroughbridge the old man found that rumour, racing ahead like a fell fire, had brought scores of curious people riding into town from as far afield as Harrogate and Easingwold. And the rumours were extraordinary. Even Peter, whose life's philosophy was based on seizing fortune by the forelock and never looking a gift horse in the mouth, was genuinely bewildered by them. They seemed to bear no relation whatsoever to the facts which were, as he saw them, that a pair of troupers were working the road down to York for the Christmastide fair. What in the name of the Giver of Gifts could that have to do with any White Bird of Kinship? Yet there was no escaping the fact that it was this which was bringing these credulous country folk flocking in.

Nor was that all. Getting a quarter out of a fell farmer was usually about as easy as pulling his teeth with your bare hands, yet here they were showering their silver into his hat as though it was chaff, and none of them thinking to dip a hand in after it either. Over a hundred royal they'd taken in three weeks, not to mention the new suit apiece that dimwitted tailor in Leyburn had insisted on making for them, refusing even a penny piece for his labour. Why, at this rate, in six months he'd have enough put by for that little pub in Kendal he'd always hankered after. Six months? A bare *three* at the pace things were going! Sure Tom couldn't grudge him that. Meanwhile here was the landlord of The Bull fingering his greasy cow-lick and trusting they would favour him with their esteemed custom. No question of *paying*! It would be his privilege. And the inn yard with its gallery would surely be ideal for their performance. It could accommodate three hundred with ease – three fifty at a pinch. The venerable Tale-Spinner had only to give word and the news would be all round the town before the church clock had struck the hour.

'All right, landlord,' said Peter magnanimously. 'But it'll cost you two royal.'

The landlord blenched, made a rapid mental calculation, and agreed.

'Two a *night*,' said Peter imperturbably. 'For the two nights.'

A slightly longer pause followed by a nod of grudging acquiescence.

'And I'll have half in advance.'

'There's my hand on it,' said the landlord, and suited the action to the word.

A wall-eyed serving wench showed them up to their room which overlooked the inn yard. 'There's a spread of clean linen,' she informed them shyly, 'and coals to the fire. Would you like that I fetch you a bite to eat?'

'Aye, lass. A meat pasty. And a jug of hot punch to help it down.'

She bobbed a half-curtsy and ducked out. Tom, who had wandered over to the window, observed that it looked as if it was going to snow.

'More than like,' said Old Peter, rubbing his hands briskly and stretching them out to the flames. 'Aren't we due a few feathers from the White Bird?' He snorted tolerantly. 'Can you make head or tail of it?'

Tom breathed on to the glass before him and drew a '3' on its side. 'I think it's like you said to Norris. People *want* to believe it. They're tired of feeling afraid.'

'But what's that got to do with *us*, lad?'

'I don't know.'

'Oh, I'll not deny you play a very pretty pipe and I tell a stirring enough tale, but what kind of sparks are they to set this sort of kindling ablaze? I tell you true, Tom, if it wasn't that we're coining money hand over fist I'd be sorely tempted to turn around and head right back to Kendal. I don't like the smell of it one bit.'

Tom moved away from the window and wandered back to the fire. 'There's nothing to be afraid of,' he said. 'I think we should go along with it.'

'Go along with what?'

'Well, tell them the story of the White Bird. You could, couldn't you?'

'And have the crows about my neck? You must be out of your mind.'

'But Morfedd said—'

'"Morfedd said!" That joker said a deal too much for your good, if you ask me! The sooner you start putting him behind you, the better for both of us. Oh, I don't mean to belittle him, lad, but we aren't in the back of beyond now, you know. Down here they're a sight more touchy about such things than they are along the Borders. And as for York . . .'

Tom regarded the old man pensively. 'I've been making up a tune to go with the White Bird,' he said. 'It's not finished yet. Would you like to hear it?'

'I suppose there's no harm. So long as it's without words. But what put that idea into your head?'

'I'm not really sure. The first bit came to me just after we left Katie. When I looked back and saw her standing there on top of the hill. Since then I've been joining things on to it. I've been using some of them for *Amulet*. That scene where the Prince meets his father's ghost is one. And there's another bit later on when he believes Princess Lorelia has been drowned. The last bit I made up at Ripon when you were telling *The Three Brothers*. Don't you remember?'

'To be honest, lad, I can't say as I do. The fact is, when I'm stuck into a tale I don't hear much above the sound of my own words. I'm hearing it and telling it at the same time. Seeing it too. In a bit of a dream I suppose you might say. Maybe that's why my tellings never come out word for word the same. Not even *Amulet*. And, blast me, if I had a silver quarter for every time I've spun *that* yarn there wouldn't be a richer man in Boroughbridge!'

Tom laughed. 'And has it always had a happy ending?'

'*Amulet*? Aye. The way I tell it. My old Dad would have the Prince dying at the end. But that cuts too close to life for my taste.'

'The White Bird dies too, doesn't it?'

'Look, do me a favour, will you, lad? Just forget about that Holy Chicken. Leastways till we're shot of York. Down south in Norwich we'll like enough get away with it, tho' even there it could still be a bit risky.'

Tom who had taken up his pipe now lowered it to his lap. 'But we're not going to Norwich,' he said. 'Just to York. That's what we agreed, wasn't it?'

'Aye, so it was,' said Peter easily. 'The fact is, Tom, I've grown so used to having you along I can't think of it being any other way. Tell me straight now, hasn't this past month been a fair old frolic? Remember that flame-headed wench at Masham, eh? Blast me but she was properly taken with you! And yon whistle wasn't the only pipe she was pining for neither! I tell you that between us we've got it made, lad! Stick with me and I swear that six months from now you'll be taking such a bag of royals home to your mam as'll topple her on the floor in a fit! You *can't* just let it drop now!'

Tom raised his pipe and slowly lowered his head above it as Peter had seen him do once before in the farmhouse kitchen. For a full minute he said nothing at all, then: 'I must go to York, Peter. I must.'

'Well, and so you shall. Show me him as says otherwise. We struck hands on it, remember? 'Sides I had word only this morning from Jack Rayner at The Duke's Arms that he's looking to us for Friday. The way I've planned it we'll just work out the Christmas fair and then you'll trot round and pay your respects to your Cousin Seymour at the Chapter House. You can't say fairer than that, can you?'

Tom nodded. 'I'm sorry,' he said. 'I really am, Peter. I think you're the finest story-teller that ever was. Listening to you is like sharing in a golden dream. But you see I promised Morfedd I'd go to York, and I can't break my promise.'

'*Morfedd*? What's he got to do with it? I thought this was all Mistress Margot's idea.'

'She thinks so,' said Tom. 'But really it was Morfedd. He planned it years ago. Long before he chose me. Before I was even *born*. It was a secret between us.'

'I'm not with you, lad. Planned *what*? That you should get yourself schooled in York Chapter? Is that supposed to make sense?'

'Oh, that's nothing to do with it. I just have to be in York at Christmas. For the forthcoming.'

'Blast it, boy, why must you speak in riddles? What "forth-coming"?'

Tom lifted his head and gazed into the flickering coals. Then in a gentle sing-song he recited: '"*The first coming was the man; the second was fire to burn him; the third was water to drown the fire, and the fourth is the Bird of Dawning.*"' So saying he took up his pipe and began to play very softly.

It seemed to the old man that the tune came drifting to him from somewhere far away like the voice of a young girl he had once heard singing on the far side of a twilit lake high up in the Apennines, strange and sweetly clear and so magical that he had scarcely dared to breathe lest he should miss a note of it. He closed his eyes, surrendering himself wholly to the enchantment.

At once there began to drift across his inward eye a series of glittering pictures that were not quite real and yet were more than mere daydreams, memories almost, of not quite forgotten moments woven into the long tapestry of years that had gone to make up his life; instants when, wholly in spite of himself, he had seemed about to reach out towards something that was at once so simple and yet so profound that he just could not bring himself to accept it. And yet it *could* be grasped because it was not outside him but within him; a vision of what might be, as when he, and he alone, by stretching out an arm in thought could wrest the deadly weapon from the uncle's hand and grant Prince Amulet life. The power was his – was *anyone*'s – was . . .

The thread of the melody snapped. Peter's eyes blinked open and the room seemed to rock into stillness around him. He felt his cloudy identity distil itself like mist on a window-pane and trickle downwards in slow, sad drops. There was a *tap-tap* at the door and, to Tom's summons, in came the serving girl bearing a tray on which was a jug and two earthenware cups and the steaming pasty which Peter had ordered. She set it down on a stool before the fire, then turned to where the boy was sitting on the edge of the bed. 'It's true what they're saying,' she whispered. 'I stood outside the door and listened. I was feared to come in while you was a-playin'.'

Tom grinned at her. 'What *are* they saying?' he asked.

'That the White Bird's a-coming. It is, isn't it?'

'Do *you* think so?'

'Aye, young master,' she said. 'I do *now*.'

*

The night before they were due to leave for York there was a heavy frost. The landlord of The Bull lit some charcoal braziers in the yard and Peter and Tom gave their final performance at Boroughbridge under a sky in which the stars seemed to quiver like dewdrops in an April cobweb. Peter was perched up on a rough dais made of planks and barrels and Tom sat cross-legged at his feet. As the recital was drawing to its close the old man caught sight of a figure slipping away from the outer fringe of the crowd. Lamplight gleamed briefly on polished metal and, a minute later, Peter's alerted ears caught the brisk and receding clatter of iron-shod hooves on cobblestones.

Later, while settling accounts with the landlord, he inquired casually whether any 'crows' had been pecking around.

The landlord glanced quickly about him, saw that they were unobserved and murmured: 'Aye, there was one.'

'Happen you know what he was seeking?'

'Not I,' said the landlord. 'He asked nowt of me.'

Peter took a bright gold half-royal out of his purse and laid it on the table between them. With his extended fingertip he nudged it delicately an inch or two towards his host. 'Flown in from York, I dare say?'

The man's eyes swivelled away from the coin and then back to it again as though tethered by an invisible thread. 'Aye, most like,' he said.

'And home to roost by starlight,' mused Peter, coaxing the coin back towards himself again. 'I wonder what sort of song he'll be croaking in the Minster?'

The landlord leant across the table and beckoned Peter closer by a tiny jerk of the head. 'Know you aught of the White Bird of Kinship, old Tale-Spinner?' he whispered.

Peter clucked his tongue, chiding ironically. 'Did you think to speak heresy with me, landlord?'

''Twas you that asked, and that's the carrion the crows are pecking for. They've smelt it blowing down strong from the hills these twelve months past. Don't tell me you've not heard the talk.'

'Aye, some to be sure. Along the Borders.'

The landlord shook his head. 'No longer. It's in the open now. Seems even the field mice have got bold all of a sudden. Me I keep my thoughts to myself.'

'So you'll live to raise wise grandsons like yourself,' said Peter, nodding approval. He tapped the coin with his fingernail. 'Was that one I saw asking after us?'

'Aye, he was. Where you hailed from. Whither bound.'

'And you told him, of course.'

'Not I. But anyone with ears in Boroughbridge could have done so. You've not kept it any close secret.'

'That's true. Well, I'm obliged to you, landlord. The boy and I have a mind to ride horseback the rest of our way. Can you manage us two hacks to The Duke's Arms in Selby Street?'

'I can that, and gladly,' said the landlord, quite at his ease once more. 'A quarter apiece they'll cost you.'

Peter nodded, opened his purse once more, joined a second half-royal to the first and pushed them across the table top. 'You'll not be out of pocket by our stay, I think.'

The landlord shrugged and pocketed the coins. 'They weren't an over-thirsty lot, but there were plenty of them.'

That night the old tale-spinner's dreams were troubled by shapes of vague ill-boding, but the shadows they cast soon lifted next morning as he urged his hired horse at a trot out of Boroughbridge along the ancient road to York. Frosty icing glittered as the early sunlight splintered off diamond sparks from the hedgerow twigs; frozen puddles crackled briskly beneath the clopping hooves; and breath of horse and rider snorted up in misty plumes along the eager nipping air.

'Hey, Tom, lad!' Peter called back over his shoulder. 'How's it feel to be entering York in style? This is the life, eh? Beats legging any day!'

Tom shook his own nag into an arthritic canter and eventually lumbered up alongside. 'No one can hear us out here, can they, Peter?'

'What about it?'

'There's something I've been wanting to ask you.'

'Well, go ahead, lad. Ask away.'

'It's about the White Bird.'

A light seemed to go out in Peter's eye. He sighed. 'Well, go on, if you must,' he said. 'Get it off your chest.'

'Just before he died Morfedd told me that the Bird *will* come down and drive the fear out of men's hearts. But he didn't say *how*. Do you know, Peter?'

'I thought I'd made it pretty clear what I think, Tom. Why don't you just let it alone, lad?'

'But you know the story, Peter.'

'I know how it *ends*,' said the old man grimly.

'The other bird, you mean?'

'Aye, lad. The Black Bird. Me, I prefer my stories to have happy endings.'

Tom rode for a while in silence considering this. 'Maybe it *was* a happy ending,' he said at last.

'Not the way I heard it, it wasn't.'

'Then maybe we should all hear it different,' said Tom. 'Perhaps that's what Morfedd meant. He said true happiness was simply not being afraid of anyone at all. He called it the last secret.'

'Did he, indeed? Well, let me tell you I'm a great respecter of Lord Fear. That's how I've lived so long. If you want to do the same you'd better start by speeding all thoughts of the White Bird clear out of your mind – or into your pipe if you must. I've more than a suspicion we'll find plenty of ears in York ready pricked for heresy, and plenty of tongues ready to run tattle with it. It's a dangerous time to be dreaming of the White Bird of Kinship, Tom. Have I made myself plain enough?'

'Aye, that you have,' said Tom and laughed cheerfully.

As they clattered over Hammerton Bridge a solitary horseman dressed in doublet and breeches of black leather, wearing a studded steel casque helmet, and with a lethal-looking metal cross-bow slung across his shoulder, emerged from behind a clump of trees and came cantering after them. 'Good morrow, strangers,' he hailed them civilly. 'You ride to York?'

'Aye, sir,' said Peter. 'To York it is.'

'For the Fairing, no doubt.'

Peted nodded.

'You buy or sell?'

The old man doffed his cap. 'A little of both, sir. Old Peter of Hereford, Tale-Spinner. At your service.'

'Well met indeed, then!' cried the bowman. 'How better to pass an hour than by sampling your goods, Old Peter. And the lad? Does he sing, or what?'

'He pipes a burden to my tales, sir.'

'A piper too, eh! Truly fortune beams upon me.' The stranger drew back his lips in a smile but his eyes remained as cold and still as slate pebbles on a river bed. 'So, what have we on offer?'

Peter rubbed his chin and chuckled. 'On such a morning as this what could suit better than a frisky love story?'

'Nay, nay, old man! I fear you might set me on so hard my saddle would come sore. I'll have none of your rutty nonsense. In truth my tastes are of a different order. Inclined more towards the fable you might say.' The smile was gone as though wiped from his face with a cloth. 'I'll have The White Bird of Kinship, Tale-Spinner, and none other.'

Peter frowned. 'Faith, sir, I'm famed to know a tale for every week I've lived, but that's a new one on me. No doubt I have it by some other name. That happens sometimes. If you could, perhaps, prompt me...'

'We'll let the lad do that for us, old rogue. Come, sprat! Put your master on the right road!'

Tom smelt old Peter's fear, rank as stale sweat, and felt a quick stab of pity for the old man. He looked across at the bowman and smiled and shook his head. 'I do have an old hill tune of that calling, sir. But it has no words to it that I know. If you wish I can finger it for you.' And without waiting for a reply he looped his reins over his pommel, dipped into his knapsack and took out his pipe.

The bowman watched, sardonic and unblinking, as the boy first set the mouthpiece to his lips then turned his head so that he was facing the newcomer directly across the forequarters of Peter's horse. Their glances met, locked, and, at the very instant of eye-contact, the boy began to play.

Whiteness exploded in the man's mind. For an appalling instant he felt the very fabric of the world rending apart. Before his eyes the sun was spinning like a crazy golden top; glittering shafts of light leapt up like sparkling spears from hedgerow and hilltop; and all about his head the air was suddenly awash with the slow, majestic beating of huge, invisible wings. He felt an almost inexpressible urge to send a wild hosanna of joy fountaining upwards in welcome while, at the same time, his heart was melting within him. He had become a tiny infant rocked in a warm cradle of wonder and borne aloft by those vast unseen pinions, up and up to join the blossoming radiance of the sun. And then, as suddenly as it had come, it was over; he was back within himself again, conscious only of a sense of desperate loss – of an enormous insatiable yearning.

The bowman sat astride his horse like one half-stunned, the

reins drooping from his nerveless fingers, while the old man turned to the boy and whispered: 'What in the name of mercy have you done to him? He looks like a sleep-walker.'

Tom ran his strange forked tongue across his upper lip. 'I thought of him like I think of the dogs,' he murmured, 'not as a man at all. Perhaps he *wanted* to believe me. Do you know who he is?'

'Aye. He's a Falcon. Each Minster has a brood of them. They have a swift and deadly swoop. I glimpsed one of them at the telling last night.' He turned back with a broad guileless smile to the bowman. 'Well, sir,' he cried cheerfully, 'now you've sampled the lad's skill, how about a taste of mine? Myself I'm in the mood for a good spicy wenching tale, if you're agreeable?'

The man nodded abstractedly and the old story-teller launched himself without further ado into a tale of lechery whose bones had been creaking long before Rome was young and yet which, for all its antiquity, lacked neither spirit nor flavour.

By the time the last score had been settled, the last knot tied, the three riders were within a strong bowshot of the city walls. Peter reined up his horse and doffed his hat with a fine flourish. 'Your servant, sir,' he said. 'And may your nights be as lively as my tale.'

The man reached absently towards the purse that hung at his belt but the old man stopped him with a lordly gesture. 'Your personal recommendation is all we crave, sir,' he said. 'We come to work the Fair.'

'So you shall have it,' said the bowman. 'I give you the word of Gyre.' He stood up in his stirrups and looked back along the road they had ridden as though he were searching for something he could no longer see. Finally he shook his head, turned back, and, glancing at Tom, said: 'I'm sorry I didn't get to hear your piping, lad. Some other time, eh?'

Tom nodded and smiled and patted the neck of his horse.

In brief salute the bowman touched his left shoulder with his clenched right fist. 'Well met, then,' he said. He shook his reins, kicked his heels into his horse's flanks and cantered off towards the west gate of the city.

As they watched him go, Peter muttered uneasily: 'Was that his idea of a joke, d'you think?'

'No,' said Tom. 'He meant it.'

'But he can't have *forgotten*.'

'I think he has,' said Tom. 'He remembers *something*, but he's not sure whether we had anything to do with it. Didn't you see him looking back along the road? Perhaps he thinks I offered to play for him and he refused.'

'And he *won't* remember?'

'I don't think so. Not unless I want him to.'

'I once knew a man in Italy who could entrance people,' said Peter. 'But he did it with words.'

Tom nodded. 'Morfedd could do that too.'

'He did it to you, did he?'

'Often.'

'And how do *you* do it?'

'I tell them too – only without words.'

'Tell them what?'

Tom looked into the old man's eyes and smiled faintly. 'I told *him* about the White Bird,' he said. 'He wanted to believe me, so it was easy.'

Peter stared at him. 'Do you *know* how you do it?'

'I know when someone wants me to.'

'But *how*, lad? What is it you *do*?'

Tom sighed faintly. 'I join myself to them. I build a bridge and walk to them over it. I take their thoughts and give them back my own.' He glanced at Peter and then away again. 'One day I'll do it for everyone, not just one or two.'

'And Morfedd taught you that, did he?'

'He taught me how to find the right keys. A different one for each person. But I believe there's a master-key, Peter. One to unlock the whole world. I call that key The White Bird.'

Peter shook his head slowly. 'Well, I'm scarcely wiser than I was before, but I'm mighty glad you did it. I had an ill vision of the two of us lying spitted at the roadside like a couple of sparrows. That little toy he carries at his back can put a bolt clean through an oak door at thirty paces.'

Tom laughed. 'I liked the story anyway.'

The old man treated him to an enormous wink. 'Come on, lad!' he cried. 'We're still alive so let's make the most of it! My throat's as dry as a brick oven.' Slapping his horse's haunch with the reins he led the way into the city.

York was the first city that Tom had ever laid eyes on. As soon as he had recovered from his initial astonishment he found it put him irresistibly in mind of an ancient oak that grew on a hillside near his home in Bowness. Known locally as the 'Wizard's Oak' this once lordly tree had been completely shattered by lightning and given up for dead. Then, a year later, it had begun to generate a few leafy shoots and, within ten years, had become a respectable living tree again. Now as he wandered about the bustling streets and squares and nosed into the dark alleys, Tom's sharp eyes picked out the dead skeleton branches of ancient York still standing amidst the new, and he found himself wondering about the race of men, long since dead and forgotten, who had erected these incredible buildings. He even conceived the odd notion that the builders must themselves have been shaped differently from ordinary men and women, not rounded but squared off and pared to sharp edges, as if their gods had first drawn them out on a plan with rule and line and then poured them into moulds, row upon row, all alike like bricks in a brick works.

Yet even underneath those stark bones he perceived faint traces of a structure yet more ancient still: great blocks of grey granite cemented into the foundations of the city's walls and, here and there, twisting flights of stone steps worn thin as wafers by the feet of generations all hurrying on to death long long ago. Once, wandering near the Minster he had seemed to sense their hungry ghosts clustering all about him, imploring him with their shadowy charnel mouths and their sightless eyes to tell them that they had not lived in vain. He had fled up on to the city walls and, gazing out across the Sea of Goole, had tried to imagine what it must have been like to live in the days before the Drowning. He strove to visualize the skies above the city filled with Morfedd's 'metal birds' and the great sea road to Doncaster thronged with glittering carts drawn by invisible horses. But in truth it was like believing that the world travelled round the sun – something you accepted because you were told it was so – and a good deal less real than many of Old Peter's tales. Even the importunate ghosts of the dead were more alive in his imagination as they came flocking greyly in upon him, unaccountable as the waves on the distant winter sea.

Staring into the setting sun, lost in time, he heard, deep within himself, yet another fragment of the melody he was always listening for. At once the smothering weight lifted from his heart. He turned, and skipping lightly down the steps, headed back to the inn.

Late on Christmas Eve a message was brought up to Clerk Seymour at the Chapter House that a man was below asking to speak with him on a matter of urgency.

The Clerk, a grey, cobwebby man with a deeply lined face and bad teeth, frowned tetchily. 'At this hour?' he protested. 'What does he want?'

'He didn't say, except that it was for your own ear.'

'Oh, very well. Send him up.'

A minute later there were steps on the wooden stairs, a deferential knock at the door and Old Peter appeared on the threshold with his hat in his hand. 'Clerk Seymour?'

'Aye, sir. And who are you?'

Old Peter closed the door carefully behind him and came forward with hand outstretched. 'Old Peter of Hereford,' he said. 'Tale-Spinner by calling. You and I are related by wedlock through my niece Margot.'

'Ah, yes. To be sure. You are bringing her boy to me. Well met, cousin.' They shook hands formally and the Clerk gestured the old man to a seat. 'I have heard many speak highly of your skill, Tale-Spinner,' he said. 'But am I not right in thinking you are over a week in York already?'

The old man made a self-deprecating gesture. 'Truly I would have called sooner,' he said, 'but I guessed these weeks would be a busy time for all at the Chapter. Is it not so?'

The Clerk smiled faintly. 'Aye, well, we are none of us idle at the Mass. That goes for you too, I dare say. You will take a cup of wine with me?'

'That I will and gladly, cousin.'

The Clerk fetched cups and a stone bottle from a cupboard. 'And how goes the Fairing for you?' he inquired amiably.

'Faith I've never known one like it,' said Peter. 'I vow I could fill Cross Square four times over and I had the voice to carry. They flock in like starlings.'

The Clerk poured out the wine carefully, re-corked the bottle, handed a cup to Peter and lifted his own in silent toast. Having taken a sip he resumed his chair. 'You are not working alone, I gather.'

'Ah, the lad you mean?' Peter nodded indulgently. 'Well, he pleaded with me to let him take a part and I hadn't the heart to deny him. He has a mighty engaging way with him has Tom. But of course you'll know that.'

'Not I,' said the Clerk. 'I've never set eyes on the boy. In truth, until Margot's letter I'd thought he was another girl. What is it he does with you?'

Peter licked a trace of wine from his lips. 'I let him pipe a burden to my tales. A snatch or two here and there. It helps things along and it keeps him happy.'

'He does it well?'

'I've had to coach him, of course. But he learns quickly. He has a good ear for a tune.'

'Then it's clear that I must make time to come and hear you.' The Clerk took another sip at his wine. 'You see the Fairing out?'

'Aye. I had thought to leg to Doncaster for the New Year but while things go so well . . .'

Clerk Seymour nodded, wondering when the old man was going to get round to saying whatever it was that he had come to say. Surely it was not just to pass the time of day? 'To Doncaster,' he murmured. 'Aye, well . . .'

Old Peter set down his cup and plucked his lower lip thoughtfully. 'Tell me, Cousin Seymour,' he said casually. 'The Chapter School. Am I right in thinking they take lads of all ages?'

'Well, within reason, yes, that is so.'

'Fourteen years would not be thought too old?'

'By no means. But surely I understood Margot to say—'

'Yes, yes,' said Peter quickly. 'Young Tom won't span fourteen for a five-month yet. What I am anxious to know, cousin, is whether his place could be held open for him till then?'

'I'm not sure that I—'

'This would be in the nature of a personal favour to me, you understand, and naturally I should be prepared to recompense the Chapter for any inconvenience it might cause.' The old man hesitated a mere half second, glanced sharply sideways and added, 'Fifty royal?'

The Clerk did his best to conceal his astonishment and did not succeed. After all, the sum mentioned was as much as he earned in a six-month! He stared at Peter. 'Forgive me, Tale-Spinner,' he said. 'But do I understand you right? You wish to postpone the boy's entry till he reaches his fourteenth year?'

Peter nodded.

The Clerk waved a hand. 'Why this, I'm sure, could easily be arranged. But *why*?'

Old Peter sank back in his chair and let out his breath in a long sigh. 'Cousin Seymour,' he said, 'you see before you an old man, friendless, alone in the world, with the final curtain about to come down upon his last act. For this month past I have found in Tom's constant companionship a source of solace and comfort I had not dreamed could be mine. My sole wish is to make one last farewell tour through the Seven Kingdoms and then back home to Cumberland and the long rest. Without Tom I could not face it. With him along it will be my crowning triumph. There now, *that* is the answer to your question.'

The Clerk nodded, pursing his lips pensively. 'And the boy? Presumably he is agreeable?'

'Oh, he loves the life! Fresh faces; fresh places. Why this last six weeks a whole new window has opened in Tom's world!'

'Then there would seem to be no problem.'

'On the face of it, you are right, cousin. But the truth of the matter is it's not quite so simple. For one thing there's still the lad's mother.'

'You mean you haven't discussed it with her?'

'Well, until the lad expressed his desire to join up with me, the question didn't arise. Since then we've got along like a house a-fire. But it's only natural he should feel a good son's duty to abide by his mother's wish.'

A gleam of belated understanding kindled in the Clerk's eye. 'Ah, I *see*,' he murmured. 'So it would suit you if we could make this delay "official"?'

Peter slipped his hand beneath his cloak, fumbled for a moment, then drew out a soft leather bag which clinked faintly as he laid it on the table. 'What harm could there be in gratifying an old man's whim, cousin? I will cherish that boy as if he were my own son. I'll even undertake to school him in his letters. And I shall return him here to you, safe and sound, before the Midsummer High Mass. All I'm asking of you is that you write a letter to Margot explaining that the place you had bespoken for the lad will not be open to him till the summer; and that when I bring Tom along here you say the same to him. That done we can all go our ways contented.'

The Clerk reached out, uncorked the wine bottle and poured out a second careful measure into the two cups. 'There is but one thing troubles me,' he said. 'I have only your word for it that the boy is happy with you. I would have to speak to him alone before I could agree.'

'You would not tell him that I have spoken with you, Cousin Seymour?'

'Naturally not,' said the Clerk, lifting his cup and touching it against Peter's. 'That is clearly understood. Nevertheless, for his mother's sake, I feel bound to insist upon it as a condition of our confidential "arrangement".'

'Agreed then,' said Peter, and with his free hand he gathered up the bag of coins and shook it gently. 'The moment you have satisfied yourself that matters are as I say, these will be yours to distribute as you think fit. To your health, cousin.'

At the very moment when the Clerk to the Chapter was chatting so amiably to the old tale-spinner, a very different sort of discussion was taking place in a tall grey tower block at the far end of the Minster Close. This building, which was known locally as 'The Falconry', was the headquarters of the whole Secular Arm of the Church Militant throughout the Seven Kingdoms. Its reputation was just as bleak as its appearance. Cold, functional, efficient; the only sign of decoration on the walls of The Falconry was an inscription in burnished steel characters riveted fast to the stonework above the main door: *Hic et Ubique*. This, when translated from its archaic tongue, read simply: 'Here and Everywhere'. Nothing further was needed.

The man responsible for overseeing all the multifarious activities of the Secular Arm had the official title of 'Chief Falconer' though he was more generally spoken of as the 'Black Bishop'. Born in 2951, the illegitimate son of a Cornish tax-collector, he had been brought up by the Black Fathers and had risen to his high eminence by dint of great intellectual ability, an outstanding capacity for organization, and an appetite for sheer hard work which had already become something of a legend before he had reached the age of twenty-five. In the seven years since he had been appointed to his present office he had completely revitalized the moribund structure he had inherited and rumour had it that his heart was set on doing the same throughout the whole of Europe. Others maintained, *sotto voce*, that here rumour lied, since it was a proven fact that the Black Bishop had no heart at all.

What he did have was a fanatical sense of dedication and a will that brooked no obstacle. It was not ambition in the commonly accepted sense of that word, rather a kind of steely conviction that he and he alone was privy to the Truth. Long ago he had been vouchsafed a vision that would have struck a responsive chord in the imagination of many a nineteenth-century engineer, for he had dreamed of the Church Militant as a vast and complex machine in which every moving part functioned to perfection, and all to the greater glory of God. In such a machine, with fallible men as its components, fear was the essential lubricant, and none knew better than the Black Bishop when and where to apply the oil can. Yet he derived no particular pleasure from watching men tremble – indeed it was debatable whether he derived particular pleasure from anything – but if he deemed it necessary he did it, and he deemed it necessary quite often.

Besides the Bishop there were four other men present in the Council Chamber high up on the fifth floor of The Falconry. They were seated two to each side of a long table. The Bishop himself sat at the head. For the past half an hour he had listened in silence while his four District Marshals gave him their verbal reports and now, with the last one concluded, he simply sat there, his left elbow resting on the arm of his chair, his chin resting on the knuckles of his left hand, and slowly looked at each of them in turn. And one by one they quailed before his eyes, their own glances seeking the shelter of the table top or the candlelit corners of the room.

'So,' he said quietly, 'I ask for facts and you bring me rumours: I ask for the firebrand and all you can offer me is a cloud of smoke. Meanwhile every road into York is choked with credulous fools hurrying in to witness the miraculous advent of . . . of *what*? A goose? A swan? A seagull? What *is* it they're expecting? Surely one of you has discovered!'

The four officers continued to stare down at the table top. Not one of them cared to risk opening his mouth.

The Bishop thrust back his chair, stood up and walked over to the wall where a map of The Seven Kingdoms was hanging. He stood for a moment, with his hands clasped behind his back, contemplating it in silence. Finally he said: 'And why here? Why

York? Why not Carlisle? Edinboro? Newcastle? Belfast, even? There must *be* a reason.'

One of the Marshals, Barran by name, observed tentatively: 'In the legend, my Lord, the White Bird —'

'Yes, yes, I know all that, Barran. Lions and unicorns. Fairy-tale nonsense. But I sense a guiding hand behind it. I feel it here, in my bones.' He turned away from the map and moved back restlessly towards his chair. 'Why do men and women *need* miracles?' he asked. 'Can any of you tell me that?'

They shook their heads.

'It is really very simple. If the life they know already is all there is for them to believe in, then most of them would be better off dead.'

The marshals' eyes widened as each one wondered whether the perilous boundary which demarcated heresy from orthodoxy was about to be re-drawn.

'It has always been so,' continued the Bishop sombrely. 'And what happens ultimately is that they are driven to create their own. Miracles born out of sheer necessity – out of spiritual starvation! Our danger is that unless we are very careful they may do it here. The time is full ripe and there are sufficient gathered for the purpose.'

'We could disperse them, my Lord.'

'You think so, Thomas? That would be a miracle indeed! By tomorrow night, at the rate things are going, they will outnumber us by hundreds to our one.'

'So many, my Lord?'

'I have it on the Mayor's authority. And there's another thing. So far there's been no whisper of civil trouble in the city. They're meek as sheep, all of them. Most have even brought in their own provisions for the week. All they do is wander up and down gawping at the Minster. Quiet as mice. Waiting. Just waiting. *But for what?*'

The Marshal called Barran cleared his throat and murmured: 'I have heard it referred to as "the forthcoming", my Lord.'

'Go on.'

'It is said that at the start of each millennium mankind is given another chance. They would have it that the Drowning in 2000 wiped the slate clean so that a new message could be written on it in the year 3000.' He tailed off apologetically and turned his hands palm upwards on the table as if to disclaim any responsibility for what he had said.

The Bishop snorted. 'The Drowning was the direct result of humanity's corporate failure to see beyond the end of its own nose. By 1985 it was already quite obvious that the global climate had been modified to the point where the polar ice caps were affected. Besides, the process itself lasted until well into the twenty-first century. Such dates are purely arbitrary.'

'But, my Lord.' Barran protested, 'the teachings of Jos—'

'Yes, yes,' cut in the Bishop irritably, 'because it suited the Church's purpose to denounce it as a Divine Judgement upon the Materialists – which of course it was. But that does not mean that the Church was not fully aware of the *physical* causes which underlay it. At the end of the twentieth century disaster could have struck in any one of a dozen different ways. By allowing us just time enough in which to adjust to it, the Drowning proved to be the most fortunate thing that could have happened. So five billions perished. When you consider the alternatives you can only allow that God was exceedingly merciful.'

The Marshals, back once more on firm ground, nodded in agreement.

'So,' said the Bishop, 'let us discard speculation and concentrate upon the practical aspects of our present situation. The one thing to be avoided at all costs is any sort of direct confrontation. The symbolic features of this ridiculous legend must on no account be permitted to gain a hold over their imaginations. Five days from now, *Deo volente*, they will all have dispersed to their homes. hopefully a good deal wiser than when they left them. In the meantime I wish our men to be seen, but nothing more. They must keep themselves in the background. Let them lend their assistance to the Civil Watch. But tell them to keep their eyes and ears open. At the first sign of anything out of the ordinary – anything which might conceivably be exaggerated into some spurious "miracle" – get word back to me *at once*, and leave it to me to decide what action should be taken. Is that understood?'

The Marshals nodded, relieved that it had been no worse.

'Have you any further questions, gentlemen?'

There were none.

Two days after Christmas Clerk Seymour sent a message to The Duke's Arms that he wished to speak with Tom. Old Peter accompanied the boy to the Chapter House. Of the two visitors there was no question who was the more nervous. Hardly had the introductions been made than Peter, pleading to afflictions of advanced age, scuttled off to relieve his bladder. It took him rather longer than might have been expected. When he re-appeared it was to learn, to his well-simulated dismay, that Tom would not be joining the Chapter School until the summer.

He clucked his tongue and shook his head dolefully, then brightened up. 'No matter, lad!' he cried. 'It's not the end of the world, is it? And the days twixt now and then will pass in an eyeblink, eh, Cousin Seymour?'

The Clerk nodded. 'I have been suggesting to Thomas that he might do a great deal worse than to keep you company on your spring travels, Tale-Spinner. Would such an arrangement be acceptable to you?'

'Nothing could please me better!' exclaimed the old man. 'Why, Tom, we'll make that round tour of the Seven Kingdoms I spoke of. That'll give you something to brag about to your school-fellows, eh? What do you say, lad?'

Tom smiled. 'It's very kind of you, Peter.'

'Pooh! Stuff!' cried the old man, clapping an arm round the boy's shoulders and hugging him tight. 'We're a team, you and I. We stand together against the world, Tom. Artists both, eh? A few days more in York then off down the high road to Doncaster. We'll follow the coast as far south as Nottingham, then, if the wind's fair, take ship to Norwich. How does that like you?'

'It likes me very well,' said Tom.

'I shall be writing to your mother, Thomas,' said the Clerk, 'to let her know that you are in good hands. As soon as you have decided what your plans are, Tale-Spinner, I will be happy to include the information in my letter. We have a Church messenger leaving for Carlisle next Wednesday. I will see that he delivers it into her own hand.'

'That's most civil of you, Cousin Seymour. Most civil.'

'Myself I depart for Malton directly,' continued the Clerk, 'but I shall be back on the eve of the New Year. Perhaps you would drop in on me then?'

'Indeed I shall. In the meantime I'll have roughed out some details of our trip.'

The Clerk accompanied them to the door of the Chapter House where they shook hands before making their way through the crowds which thronged the Minster Close. As they were passing The Falconry a man emerged from beneath the overshadowing porch and caught sight of them. He paused a moment, watching them through narrowed eyes, then ran lightly down the steps and plucked the old man by his sleeve. 'Greetings, old Tale-Spinner,' he murmured. 'Dost remember me?'

Peter turned. 'Aye, sir,' he said. 'Even without the casque. How goes it with you, Falcon Gyre?'

The man glanced back over his shoulder. 'I was at the telling last night,' he said.

'I am indeed honoured,' returned Peter, with the merest hint of irony in his voice. 'Didst prefer it to the other?'

'I would talk with you, old man. But not here.'

Peter flicked a quick glance at Tom who appeared supremely unconcerned. 'Aye, well,' he muttered uneasily. ''Tis not the best of times, friend Gyre. We have a telling billed within the hour. Would not tomorrow be —'

'Tomorrow would be too late,' said Gyre, 'I know of a place hard by.' As he spoke he tightened his grip perceptibly on the old man's arm and steered him, gently but firmly, towards a narrow alley.

By a series of twists and turns they were conducted into a courtyard which fronted on to a backstreet market. There in a dingy shop which was part alehouse, part general store, Gyre ordered up three mugs of spiced wine, guided the old man and the boy into a corner settle and said: 'You must quit York tonight.'

For some seconds Peter was too taken aback to say anything at all, then he managed to stutter: 'By whose authority comes this? We break no law.'

Gyre shook his head. 'I, Gyre, tell you this, old man. For three nights past I have had the same dream. I wish no harm to befall you. Stay not in York.' He spoke in little impetuous rushes, like one who has run hard and snatches for his breath.

Old Peter gazed at him, noted the unnatural brightness of eyes which he had first seen cold as the pennies on a dead man's sockets, and he remembered the way this licensed bird of prey had stood up in his stirrups and stared back along the sunlit road to Hammerton Bridge. 'A dream, eh, friend?' he murmured mildly. 'And three nights running. Is that all you can tell us?'

Gyre looked from the old man to the boy and back again. 'I

noose my own neck by speaking of it with you,' he said. 'Will you not be warned?'

'Aye, man, we are truly grateful. Think not otherwise. But this dream of yours. Could it not have some other reading?'

'Perhaps,' said Gyre, and all the urgency had suddenly drained from his voice. He sounded almost indifferent.

'You cannot tell us?'

'It comes and goes again,' said Gyre and frowned. 'I know when it has been, but I know nothing of its nature.'

'And yet you sought us out to warn us?'

'Aye, well.' Gyre shrugged. 'Something came over me.' He got up and, without another word to them, walked out of the shop and disappeared, leaving his drink untasted on the table.

Old Peter stared after him, kneading his chin with his thumb knuckle. 'What make you of that?' he asked.

'He meant it,' said Tom.

'Yes. But meant *what*, lad? Did you see his eyes?'

Tom sipped his drink and said nothing.

'I'll warrant he'd been chewing 'drasil root.'

'But we could go, couldn't we, Peter? We don't have to stay now, do we?'

'Ah, you're forgetting your Cousin Seymour. He won't be back from Malton till Monday. Besides, lad, this place is a regular gold mine for us. Close on twenty royal a day we're taking. A *day*! And I can recall plenty of times when I've not taken one in a week!'

'All right,' said Tom. 'So we'll stay.'

'Me I'm not superstitious,' said Peter. 'I can't afford to be. Still I wouldn't like you to feel that I . . .'

Tom laughed. 'And abandon a gold mine? Never!'

'Ah, I thought you'd see it my way,' said Peter complacently, and catching up Gyre's abandoned mug he swigged it off in a single draught.

At the tenth hour of the New Year's Eve, Old Peter shrugged on his heavy cloak and set out to keep his appointment at the Chapter House. That afternoon he had totted up the sum of their takings over the past fortnight and found it came to the staggering total of 178 royal. Even allowing for the fifty he had pledged to the Clerk this was still a golden harvest the like of which he had never known. It had driven him, for the first time in his life, to seek the services of the bankers. Now, folded flat and stowed away in a concealed pocket within the lining of his doublet, he carried a letter of credit which would see them both round the Seven Kingdoms and back again to York even if they never took another quarter. Truly, as far as Peter was concerned, the advent of the millennium had already proved wholly miraculous.

As he approached the Chapter House he was astonished to find the Minster Close almost deserted. On this night of all nights he had expected to see the crowds milling in readiness to celebrate the midnight chimes. Then he recalled how an Order had been promulgated from The Falconry that very morning banning all such gatherings within the city walls on account of a case of plague which had been discovered. He looked about him. Over the roofs to the south he saw the low clouds already tinted a coppery red from the flames of invisible bonfires that had presumably been kindled on the open ground beyond the southern gate. He decided that as soon as his business with the Clerk was concluded he would take a stroll along the walls to watch the sport.

He was kept waiting for a cold half hour at the Chapter House before Clerk Seymour could receive him and by the time all the details of the transaction had been settled, the cash handed over and a pledge drunk in wine, the last half-hour chime before midnight was sounding from the Minster. Peter stepped back out into the night to find that the air had become alive with snowflakes, large and soft as swansdown. There was no wind at all, and where the two wall torches flamed beside the entrance to The Falconry the currents of rising air were setting the drifting flakes into a swirling dance like twin clouds of golden moths.

As the old man hefted up the hood of his cloak and re-tied the leather laces at his chin a solitary horseman came spurring into the Close. He reined up outside The Falconry, flung himself from the saddle and, without even bothering to tether his mount, raced up the steps and into the building. Reflecting that no news travels faster than bad news, Peter made haste to quit the scene. He was hurrying towards the southern gate when a troop of five Falcons, helmeted and with their bows at their backs, galloped past him down the main street, the steel-shod hoofs of their horses striking showers of sparks from the snow-slippery cobblestones. So uncannily silent was the town that Peter could hear their clattering racket long after they had passed out of his sight.

The last quarter-chime had just died on the air as he set foot on one of the ancient stairways that led up to the top of the city wall. Pausing to gather breath for the climb, the old man suddenly remembered Tom. The thought came to him in the form of a brilliantly clear mental image of the boy's face as he had once seen it lit up by the flamelight from Norris's hearth. As if a hand had been thrust violently into his back, the old man began scrambling up the stairs two at a time. Heart pounding, lungs wheezing like a blacksmith's bellows, he staggered up on to the battlements and peered dizzily over. The sight that met his eyes all but brought his heart to a full stop. By the light of a dozen bonfires an enormous crowd was assembled, a silent sea of blank white faces gazing upwards towards the city wall. The only sound to be heard was the crackle of flames as a log broke in two and a fountain of sparks swept up to meet the ceaseless downward sift of the snowflakes. The *only* sound? 'Dear God,' groaned the old man in what was part prayer, part incantation, 'Dear God, no.'

He set off in a shambling, broken-winded run along the battlements, pausing every now and again to peer downwards. He came upon other silent watchers, first in ones and twos, then clustered ever more closely together, leaning over the parapet, rapt and still. He elbowed his way between two of them and saw that a little way below and some thirty paces to his right, a rough wooden scaffold had been erected by masons working to repair an inward-curving section of the wall. A ladder led down from the parapet to a boarded platform, and there, seated so casually that one leg hung dangling over the airy gulf below, was Tom. His back resting against a rough pine joist, the snow already beginning to settle unheeded upon his bent head, he was playing his lament for The White Bird of Kinship; playing it really for nobody but himself, unless perhaps it was for the spirit of a man he had once loved who had dreamed an impossible dream of human kinship long ago among the hills and valleys of Bowness.

As Peter stared downwards it seemed to him that the whole scene was becoming oddly insubstantial: the pale upturned faces of the silent crowd beginning to swirl and mingle with the drift and swirl of the pale flakes; the stones along the parapet touched with the rosy firelight until they appeared to glow with the warm inward glow of molten glass. All about him he seemed to sense a world becoming subtly transformed into something wholly new and strange, yet a part of him still realized that this transformation must lie within his own perception, within himself.

– I believe there's a master-key, Peter. One to unlock the whole world. I call that key The White Bird.

As the boy's words came whispering back into his memory an extraordinary excitement gripped the old man. Fear slipped from him like a dusty cloak. He began to hear each separate note of the pipe as clearly as if Tom were sitting playing at his side and he knew that every listener in that vast concourse was hearing the same. So it was that, despite himself, no longer caring, Peter found his head had tilted backwards until the feathery snowflakes came drifting down upon his own upturned face. And gradually, as he surrendered himself to the song, he too began to hear what Gyre had once heard – the great surging downrush of huge wings whose enormous beat was the very pulse of his own heart, the pulse of life itself. He felt himself being lifted up to meet them as if he were being rushed onwards faster and faster along some immense and airy avenue of cool white light. Of their own accord his arms rose, reached out in supplication, pleading silently – *Take me with you . . . take me . . . take me . . .* But, ah, how faint they were becoming, how faint and far away. Ghostly wingbeats sighing fainter and ever fainter, washed backwards by an ebbing sky-tide, drifting beyond his reach far out over the distant southern sea. Away. Gone away. Gone.

The old tale-spinner opened his eyes without realizing that he had ever closed them. What had happened? There was a mysterious sighing in the air, an exhalation, as if the held breath of the whole world had been released. *Gone away. Gone. Our bird. Our own White Bird. Why hast thou forsaken us?* He shook his head like a wet dog and blinked round at the vacant, dream-drugged faces beside him. And it was then that he realized the music had stopped. A sound most like an animal's inarticulate bewildered growl broke from his throat. He lunged forward, thrust himself half over the parapet and squinted down through the lazily drifting petals of the indifferent snow.

The boy was lying, head slumped, limbs twisted askew on the wooden platform. Through the left side of his chest a single crossbow bolt fledged with ravens' feathers was skewering him to the pine joist behind him. One hand was still clutched around the projecting shaft of the bolt as if to pull it free. On the snowy boards blood was already spreading outwards in a slow, dim puddle.

Forcing his way through the press of stunned spectators the old man gained the ladder by which Tom must have descended and, heedless of his own safety, clambered down to the platform. As he set foot on it the Minster bells suddenly unleashed their first great clamorous peal, flighting out the Old Year and welcoming in the New.

Accompanied by Marshal Barran the Chief Falconer strode furiously along the top of the city wall. In the distance he could make out a little huddled knot of onlookers, lit by flickering torch light, gathered around the top of the scaffolding. Down in the meadows below, the mounted troopers were already dispersing the crowd. For the third time he asked the same question: 'And you are absolutely *certain* this was the same boy?'

'There could not be two such, my Lord. He fits the Boroughbridge report perfectly.'

'Insane,' muttered the Bishop. 'Absolutely insane. Whose troop is the madman in?'

'Dalkeith's, my Lord.'

'And why *that* way when he could have slit the pup's throat in a back alley and no one a wit the wiser? Now we've got ourselves five thousand eyewitnesses to a needless martyrdom. And on this one night of all nights!'

'Aye, my Lord. They're already murmuring about the Black Bird.'

'And for how long do you suppose it will stay a murmur? In a month they'll be shouting it from the rooftops. What they'll be saying by this time next year is anybody's guess.'

Already the snow was falling more heavily and a breeze had sprung up, blowing in from the sea, bringing the smoke from the dying bonfires billowing up along the battlements. Two members of the Civil Watch had found a plank, had laid the boy's body upon it. Having covered it with a piece of sacking, they were now arguing about how best to get it down the narrow steps. The Chief Falconer strode into the centre of the group. 'Back!' he commanded.

As they shuffled to obey he stooped over the makeshift bier, twitched aside the sacking and stared down at the pale calm face of the dead boy. He caught sight of a leather lace about the throat and, thinking it might be a crucifix, jerked it clear. All he found was a bloody fragment of a shattered green pebble. 'The bolt,' he said. 'Where is the bolt?'

'I have it safe,' said a voice from the shadows.

The Bishop raised his cowled head and peered into the shadows. 'Who are you?'

'Peter of Hereford. Tale-Spinner. He was my lad.'

Marshal Barran leant across and whispered something into the Bishop's ear. The Chief Falconer frowned. 'What know you of this sad accident, Peter?'

The old man stepped forward into the pool of quivering torchlight. From beneath his cloak he produced the black-fledged bolt, its crumpled feathers already stiff with congealed blood. 'This was an accident, sire?' he said. 'Your birds flew here this night to shed innocent blood.'

'Have a care for your tongue, old man.'

'Fear you the truth, my Lord Bishop? Know then there should by rights have been two of us down there. I to tell the tale and he to breathe the breath of life into it. Ask any man or woman who heard Tom play whether or not the White Bird of Kinship hovered here tonight.'

The Bishop glanced swiftly round at the circle of impassive faces and felt suddenly as if the sea wind was blowing right through his bones. Why was this old scoundrel not afraid to speak these heresies to his face? Men had been racked to death for less. Something was stirring here that even he might well be powerless to quell. There was a rank smell of false faith in the air. Well at least there would be no more public martyrdoms this night. He touched the bier with his foot. 'Get this down to the gatehouse. As for you, Tale-Spinner, present yourself at The Falconry by the tenth hour of forenoon. Meanwhile you would be well advised to place a closer guard over that precious tongue of yours.'

The snow stopped shortly after dawn. When Peter made his way to The Falconry next morning it was through streets muffled as if on purpose to honour the dead. Everywhere along his route people, recognizing him, came up and touched hands and went away. Few said more than: 'I was there', but their eyes were eloquent.

The ghost of an old fear brushed against him as he mounted the snowy steps to The Falconry but it no longer had the same power to freeze him from the inside out. He strode into the building, stamped the ice from his boots and told the doorkeeper who he was. The man directed him down an echoing passage into a room where a log fire was burning. Crouched on a stool beside the fire was Falcon Gyre.

Peter gazed at the bowman in surprise then walked across and placed a hand on his shoulder. 'Well met, friend,' he murmured. 'Would that we had heeded those dreams of yours.'

Gyre looked up but there was no hint of recognition in his eyes. They seemed to look right through the old man to something far beyond that only he could see. Peter remembered how he had stared back along the sunlit road across the moors to Hammerton and wondered what thoughts were going through his mind. 'You did your best, friend,' he said. 'No one could have done more.'

As though by a superhuman effort Gyre brought his eyes to focus on the face above him. His lips trembled loosely and, suddenly, with a shock of real pity, Peter saw the man was weeping silently, the tears runnelling down his unshaven cheeks and dripping unheeded from his chin. At that moment the door opened and the Chief Falconer walked in. He stood for a moment gazing with obvious distaste at the blubbering Gyre, then he turned to Peter and said: 'What do you wish done with him?'

Peter glanced round, half convinced that the Bishop was addressing someone else in the room whom he had not yet seen. 'I?' he protested. 'Why should I . . .?'

'He has not told you?'

'He has not spoken a word. I thought perhaps he was . . .'

'He is in a state of profound shock,' said the Bishop. 'He remembers nothing. Nevertheless he was responsible for the accidental death of the boy.'

'*Gyre!* Never!'

'So you know his name?'

'Aye. We rode into York together. My Lord, I assure you there has been some mistake. This cannot be the man.'

'There has been no mistake,' said the Bishop testily. 'Gyre loosed the bolt by accident. Think you we would have *ordered* him to do it? Surely even you must have the wit to realize that it was the last thing on earth we could have wished.'

Peter stared down at the silently weeping man and then back to the Bishop. 'No man could have fired that shot by accident,' he said slowly. 'It would have been difficult even for a skilled marksman. Upwards – against the falling snow – with only the firelight to aim by? That was no accident. But whoever did it it was not Gyre.'

The Bishop drew his lips back against his teeth with a faint sucking sound. 'And just what makes you so certain?' he asked curiously.

Peter shrugged. What had either of them to lose by it now? 'Because Gyre tried to warn us to leave the city three days ago.'

'*Warn you?* How?'

'He told us to quit York. He said he had had a dream.'

The Bishop gazed at the old man, seeing the ripples of superstition multiplying, crowding thick upon each other, ringing outwards wider and wider with every minute that passed. 'A dream,' he said flatly. 'What dream?'

'He would not tell us. But he said he had the same dream three nights running. He just warned us to leave. Would to God we'd listened to him. But I had arrangements still to make with the Chapter Clerk for the lad's schooling.'

'Schooling?' echoed the Bishop. 'Are you telling me the boy was to enter the Chapter School?'

'Aye, my Lord. That's why I brought him here to York.'

'But in that case he was certainly destined for the Ministry.'

'I know naught of that, my Lord.'

The Bishop punched one hand into the other. 'Oh, he was, he was,' he said. 'There can be no question of it. Besides, the Clerk will certainly confirm it. You must realize that this puts a very different complexion on the matter.'

'How so, my Lord?'

'Why naturally he must be interred in the Minster crypt with all due honour as befits a true son of the Church. How like you that, old man? Better than a public grave in the wall ditch, wouldn't you say?'

Peter looked hard at him. 'I dare say Tom will not be minding much either way,' he said. 'But make it a grave in the open Close if you must. Those Minster stones would lie too heavy on his heart.'

'So be it,' said the Bishop. 'Leave it to us, old man. I promise you he shall lack for nothing.'

'Except a little breath, my Lord.'

Frost laid an icy finger on the Bishop's smile. 'Have a care,' he murmured, 'or that golden tongue of yours may buy a grave of your own.'

And so it came to pass that on the third day of the New Year the Minster bells rang out once more. The pine coffin, decked with blood-berried holly, was borne from the gatehouse through the twisting streets to the doors of the Minster and vanished inside. By the time it re-emerged the crowd of mourners in the Close had swollen beyond computation, lapping out even to engulf the steps of the Falconry itself.

Gazing down sombrely from his fifth floor eyrie the Chief Falconer was moved to question his own wisdom in acceding to the old man's wish that the body be buried outside the Minster. Where had they all appeared from, these massed ranks of silent watchers? What marvellous sign were the fools hoping for? He watched with growing impatience as the bearers made their slow way through the crowd towards the heap of upturned earth beside the newly dug grave. As they laid the coffin across the leather straps, the first feathery flake of new snowfall came drifting downwards outside the window. Another followed and another, and then the Bishop saw faces here and there in the throng lift and gaze upwards. In less than a minute only the officiating clergy appeared concerned in the burial, the rest were reaching upwards, hands outstretched in supplication towards this miraculous manna softly falling feathers of the immortal White Bird of Kinship whose song once heard would never be forgotten.

The Bishop turned to Marshal Barran with a mirthless smile. 'I suppose you realize that it is more than likely we are witnessing a future miracle.'

Barran nodded. 'You did well, my Lord, to claim him for the Church. Think what this might have become had it taken place below the city walls.'

'I hope you're right,' said the Chief Falconer. 'Myself I'm not so sure. What if this fledgeling we've taken into our nest should prove to be a cuckoo?'

Barran returned his attention to the scene below just in time to see the coffin disappear jerkily out of sight. The priest scattered a handful of soil into the grave and stepped back. As he did so those nearest to the graveside shuffled forward and each appeared to drop something white on to the lid of the hidden coffin. Soon a long procession had formed. As it wound slowly past the heap of raw earth each man, woman and child stretched out an arm and dropped a single white feather into the open grave.

Barran debated whether to draw the Bishop's attention to this new development and decided against it. Instead, he remarked: 'Do you recall, my Lord, how the fable ends?'

'With the death of the bird, of course.'

'Oh no, my Lord. They would have it that when the blood of the dying white bird splashes the breast of the black, then the black bird becomes white itself and the cycle is repeated.'

The Bishop swung round on his Marshal, his eyes seeming to smoulder like dark red coals. 'In God's name, Barran, don't you see what you're saying? Why didn't you tell me this before?'

'My Lord,' stammered the Marshal, 'indeed I would have done so, but you assured me you were familiar with the legend. As I recall it you —'

'Aye, man, I remember. Lions and unicorns I called it. Stupid fairy tale nonsense. Well, so it is. So are they all. Credulous idiots. Children. Fools.' He sighed. 'Ah, well, it's done now – for better or worse. I only wish I could believe it was for the better.'

Standing beside the grave, with the snow falling all about him, a lone piper had begun to play a hauntingly familiar lament.

'Amen to that, my Lord,' murmured the Marshal.

Three days after the funeral two men rode out of the city by the south gate and took the shore road for Doncaster. One rider was Old Peter of Hereford; the other an ex-Falcon by the name of Gyre. Around Gyre's neck was fastened a thick hinged band of studded brass clamped at the throat by a steel padlock. The key to this lock was in Old Peter's purse. The Collar of Servitude was the punishment which, as near kin, he had elected at the behest of the Secular Court; the rejected alternative would have been ritual blinding with a white-hot iron.

When they were some fifteen kilometres clear of the city, Old Peter signalled Gyre to dismount then climbed down off his own horse. He beckoned the Falcon to him, unlocked the brass collar and flung it far out into the Sea of Goole. The key followed it.

'That's the way Tom would have wanted it,' said the old man, panting from his exertions. 'You're free, Gyre.'

Gyre, who had spoken no intelligible word to anyone since loosing the fatal bolt, produced a sort of bubbling gurgle from deep inside his throat. Then he turned away, went back to his horse and unfastened one of the leather saddlebags. From inside it he took out something wrapped in a piece of blue cloth which he brought to Peter.

'What's this?' said the old man. 'An exchange, eh?' He unwrapped the cloth and then drew in his breath in a painful hiss. 'Man, how came you by this?'

Gyre looked down at the pipe which the Wizard of Bowness had fashioned for Tom and then he laid his clasped hands against his chest and crouched down in the damp sand at the water's edge and whimpered like a dog.

'Why did you do it, Gyre?' muttered the old man. 'What made you, man?'

Gyre raised his head, unclasped his hands, and with his right forefinger gently touched the barrel of the pipe. As he did so the sun thrust aside the clouds and shone down upon him. An expression of childlike wonder softened his ravaged face. His fingers closed round the pipe, eased it from the old man's grasp, and then set it to his own lips. Closing his eyes he blew gently down it and then began to move his fingers falteringly over the stops.

To his dumb amazement the old man heard the unmistakable air of one of the themes which Tom had first devised for *Amulet* and then incorporated into his Lament for the White Bird. Gyre played it all through once, and then again, gaining assurance as he proceeded. As Peter listened in a sort of trance, understanding broke over him in a foaming wave of revelation. It was as though the music had brought him the answer to his own question. And it lay back there behind him on a road fifteen kilometres to the northward where the boy had once said to him in that quiet, supremely confident way of his – 'I told *him* about the White Bird. He wanted to believe me, so it was easy.' But what was it you had wanted to believe, Gyre? That the Bird was a living reality which would indeed come winging out of the winter sky? If you believed that, then you would have to believe all the rest too. Which meant believing that the Bird *must* die in order to live again!

111

Like bright bubbles rising to the swirling surface, memories began to cluster together in the old man's mind; remembered things that Tom had said: 'They are such ninnies they'll believe anything' – 'I thought of him like I think of the dogs, not as a man at all' – 'I take their thoughts and give them back my own'. And others too: 'Our thoughts are unseen hands shaping the people we meet' – 'Morfedd planned it all years ago. Long before he chose me. Before I was even born.' The old man began to shiver right deep down in the very marrow of his bones. What manner of being had this boy been? What latent power in him had Morfedd recognized and nurtured? Was it possible Tom could have *known* what he was about – or even *half* known – enough to stamp a picture of his own destiny on Gyre's too willing mind? *Could he have chosen his own death?* Every instinctive fibre in Peter's being rejected the notion. And yet . . . and yet . . . the pattern would not go away. One by one the nails thudded into the coffin and among the hands wielding the hammers one was his own. 'I thought you'd see it my way.' *Thud!* 'A few more days in York then off down the high road to Doncaster.' *Thud!* 'You're forgetting your Cousin Seymour. He won't be back from Malton till Monday.' *Thud!* 'What harm could there be in gratifying an old man's whim, cousin?' *Thud!* Nailed down by the strength of an old man's weakness. That collar should have been round his own neck not Gyre's. With everything to lose, poor crazed Gyre had at least seen the boy as an end in himself. 'I, Gyre, tell you this. I know when it has been but I know nothing of its nature.' Why was it that men could never value things truly till they were gone?

Far out to sea a ship with silver-white sails was dipping and plunging in and out of the slanting shafts of sunlight. Eagerly the blue-grey waves hurried in, stumbled, and creamed up the gently shelving beach as they had done for a thousand years. The old tale-spinner looked down at the man still crouched at his feet. A huge calmness descended upon him. He stretched out his arm and gripped Gyre gently by the shoulder. Then he walked down to the water's edge and dipped both his hands into the sea. Returning he tilted back Gyre's head and with a wet finger drew across his forehead the sign that Tom had once drawn on a misty window of an inn – a child's representation of a flying bird. 'Come friend,' he said. 'You and I together have a tale to tell. Let us be on our way.'

112

The Hertford Manuscript

The death of my Great Aunt Victoria at the advanced age of ninety-three lopped off the longest branch of a family tree whose roots have been traced right back to the fifteenth century – indeed, for those who are prepared to accept 'Decressie' as a bona fide corruption of 'de Crècy', well beyond that. Talking to my aunt towards the end of her life was rather like turning the pages of a Victorian family album, for as she grew older the England of her childhood seemed to glow ever more brightly in her mind's eye. In those far-off days it had been fashionable to accept the inevitability of human progress with a wholehearted-ness which is almost impossible for us to imagine. In the 1890s life presented *homo sapiens* with a series of 'problems' which had to be 'solved'. It was as simple as that. The Edwardians merely gilded the roof of that towering pagoda of Victorian optimism which collapsed in smithereens in 1914.

James Wilkins – Great Aunt Victoria's husband – died of trench fever in the Dardanelles in 1916. They had no children and she never married again. I learnt later from my aunt that James had been a keen member of the Fabian Society. He had also been an active partner in the antiquarian book business of Benham & Wilkins which owned premises off Old Bond Street.

Shortly after James's death, and much to her family's astonishment, Victoria announced her intention of taking over her husband's share of the business. She very soon proved herself to be an extremely capable business woman. She made a speciality of English incunabula and throughout the twenties and thirties she built up a thriving trade with countless museums and university libraries all over the world. When the vast Hertford Collection was sold off to pay death duties in 1938, Great Aunt Victoria had her seat reserved in the front row of the auction gallery throughout the two weeks of the sale, and in the price register published afterwards the name 'Wilkins' was prominent among the list of buyers.

In October 1940 a direct hit from an incendiary bomb destroyed the premises and much of the stock of Benham & Wilkins overnight. It also seemed to destroy something in Aunt Victoria herself. She was close on sixty at the time, living alone in Hampstead, and I remember receiving a letter from her in which she told me that she had decided to sell out. She did not sound particularly regretful about it. 'No doubt it had to happen,' she wrote, 'and I consider myself fortunate that it did not happen to me too.' I discounted the unfamiliar note of fatalism in her words as being due to shock.

She lived on in her house in Well Walk, growing perceptibly frailer as the years advanced, but with her mind still alert and sharp. I used to make a point of calling in to see her whenever I was up in Town and was invariably offered China tea and caraway-seed cake, for which she had a life-long passion. On one occasion, in the late fifties, she told me she had once been 'propositioned' by H. G. Wells.

'I had no idea you knew him,' I said. 'When was that?'

'Oh, at about the time he and Shaw and the Webbs were squabbling over the future of the Society.'

'The Fabian Society?'

'Yes, of course. 1907 I think it was.'

'And what was the proposition?'

She laughed. 'The usual one, I gathered. He said he wished me to help him with a book he was writing on the emancipation of women.' She paused and gazed out of the window. 'He was a strangely attractive little man.'

'But you didn't accept?'

'No. Perhaps I should have done. Of course I had met him before that – at the Huxleys. Everyone was talking about him.' She paused again and seemed for a while to lose herself in reverie, then she remarked: 'Did you ever read a story of his called "The Chronic Argonauts"?'

'I can't recall it,' I said. 'What was it about?'

'About a man who invents a machine which will carry him through Time.'

'Oh, you mean "The Time Machine", Aunt.'

'Indeed I don't. I'm quite sure that was the title. I'd never seen "chronic" used in that way before. It was a serial he was writing for a magazine. He showed me a copy of the first instalment. You see we both knew the man it was based on.'

'I'm surprised it was based on anyone,' I said.

'Oh, yes,' she assured me. 'A Doctor Robert Pensley. He lived in Herne Hill. Like all of us in those days he too was a great admirer of Professor Huxley.'

I helped myself to another slice of seed cake. 'And what did the Doctor make of young Wells's portrait of him?' I asked.

'As far as I know he never read it.'

'Oh? Why not?'

'He disappeared.'

I blinked at her. 'Just like that?'

She nodded. 'It created quite a stir at the time. There were rumours that he had skipped off to America.'

'And had he?'

'*I* don't think so. And neither did Wells.' She chuckled – a strangely youthful sound from lips so old – and added: 'I remember H.G.'s very first words to me when he learnt what had happened: "By God, Vikki, don't you see? He's done it!"'

'And what did he mean by that?' I asked.

'Travelled in Time, of course,' said Aunt Victoria in the matter-of-fact tone she might have employed in saying: 'Caught the ten-fifteen to Portsmouth.'

I am ashamed to say I laughed.

She gave me a darting, sidelong glance from her clear, grey eyes. 'You think it quite impossible, of course.'

'Oh, quite,' I said, setting down my tea cup and wiping the cake crumbs from my fingers with my handkerchief.

'Wells didn't think so.'

'Ah, yes,' I said. 'But then he wrote science-fiction, didn't he?'

'I don't see what that has to do with it.'

'Well, I presume he'd just appreciated that he had the material for an excellent story. After all, he wrote it, didn't he?'

'He wrote it *down*,' she said.

'Well, there you are then. And no doubt Doctor Pensley's descendants are living happily in America to this day.'

Aunt Victoria smiled faintly and let the subject drop.

I was in Melbourne, Australia, right on the other side of the globe, when I received a letter telling me that Aunt Victoria had died. The news did not come as any great surprise because I knew she had been in poor health ever since catching a severe dose of 'flu in the early spring, but the sense of loss I felt was real enough. Her death seemed to nudge me appreciably nearer to my own grave.

When I returned home to England, some six weeks later, it was to discover that my aunt's mortal remains were nourishing the rose bushes in Highford cemetery and the house in Well Walk had already been sold. I also discovered a letter awaiting me. It was signed by her Bank Manager, who, it appeared, was the Executor of her will, and it informed me that I had been left a legacy of a thousand pounds together with 'a particular token of the regard in which the late Mrs Wilkins held you.'

I lost no time in travelling up to Town from my house in Bristol and presenting myself at the Bank Manager's office. After the formal exchange of polite regrets for the sad nature of the occasion I was handed a brown paper parcel, securely tied and sealed, with my own name written upon it in Aunt Victoria's quite remarkably firm hand. I signed the official receipt, was presented with an envelope containing a cheque for £1,000, and stepped out into the street. I was not consumed by any over-whelming curiosity to discover exactly what 'token of regard' the parcel contained. From the shape of it I guessed that it must be a book of some kind and I had a shrewd suspicion that it would prove to be the photograph album which Aunt Victoria and I had often looked at together when I visited her in Well Walk.

There being nothing further to detain me in London I took a taxi to Paddington and caught the first available train back to Bristol. Having decided to invest a modest portion of my windfall on a first-class ticket I had the unfamiliar luxury of a whole compartment to myself and, seated there, relaxed and extremely pleased with myself and the world, I finally got round to untying the string which, I did not doubt, Aunt Victoria had fastened with her own capable hands.

I soon realized that I had been mistaken in my previous assumption. The book which emerged from beneath the layers of brown paper and newsprint in which it was wrapped had certainly been old long before the invention of photography. It measured roughly 12 inches by 9 inches, was bound in dark brown leather, and had a heavily ridged spine of the kind which I believe is known in the antiquarian book trade as 'knuckled'. There was no tooling of any kind either on the covers or on the

116

spine, in fact nothing at all on the outside of the book to indicate what its contents might be. For the life of me I could not conceive why Aunt Victoria should have left it to me.

As I turned back the front cover I found, lying inside, a sealed envelope, inscribed with my Christian name and bearing at the bottom right hand corner a date – '4 June 1958'.

I laid the book down on the seat beside me, slit open the envelope and extracted two sheets of the tinted notepaper which my aunt had always favoured. I put on my spectacles and read the following:

Wednesday evening

My dear Francis,
There was a point during our conversation this afternoon when I was sorely tempted to march upstairs and fetch down this book. Though I am sure you don't realize it there was something about the way in which you dismissed the very idea of time travel as being 'Quite impossible!' that struck me as almost unbearably smug. However, second thoughts being, as usual, better than first impulses, I have decided instead that I shall leave you the book in my will. So by the time you read this letter I dare say you will already have become accustomed to thinking of me as your late Aunt rather than your Great Aunt! I confess that it makes me smile even as I write it.

From the ex-libris plate inside the front cover you will see that this book comes from the Hertford Library which was sold up in 1938. It was part of a lot consisting of some half a dozen miscellaneous seventeenth-century Registers which I obtained for the proverbial song simply because no one else seemed interested in them. It was not until I was going through them to make out entries for our Overseas catalogue that I noticed that one of them had stitched into the back of it about twenty flimsy sheets of paper which were quite different in texture from those which make up the rest of the volume. Since the binding itself was indisputably seventeenth-century workmanship and all the other entries concerned the years 1662–1665, I started to examine these odd pages with some interest. I discovered, to my astonishment, that they constituted a sort of rough journal or diary, written in pencil, and covering a period of some three weeks in August and September 1665.

I will not spoil my own pleasure in imagining your expression as you read them by telling you what I believe them to be. All I *will* say is that the Register was entered in the Hertford Catalogue in 1808 as having been purchased along with two others 'from the Estate of

Jonas Smiley Esq.' To the very best of my knowledge they lay there in the library of Hertford Castle quietly gathering dust for the next 130 years.

I trust you will find it as interesting and as instructive as I did.
Yours most affectionately,

Victoria

I re-read the letter from beginning to end in total bewilderment. At first, I confess, I could only assume that I was the victim of some extraordinary practical joke she had chosen to play upon me, but it was so *unlike* Aunt Victoria to do anything of the kind that, in the end, I simply shrugged and picked up the book. Sure enough, pasted inside the front cover was an engraved bookplate depicting two remarkably well-developed mermaids holding aloft a shell in which reclined a grinning skull, a quill pen and an hour glass. Circumscribing this somewhat ill-assorted gathering was a fluttering banner emblazoned with the legend *EX LIBRIS HERTFORDENS* so at least there seemed to be no doubt about that part of Aunt Victoria's story. I turned over the stained flyleaf and found myself contemplating an ornate sepia script which informed me that this was yᵉ Register opened on November 20th 1662 for yᵉ Hostel of Saint Barnabas in yᵉ Parish of Wapping of which yᵉ Recording Clerk was one Tobias Gurney. The first entry on the next page read: '*Decd. at the 4th hr. Agnes Miller, fem. age indet. of yᵉ fev. quot. tert.*'

I ran my eye down the column which appeared to consist almost entirely of records of deaths, and then flicked on through the yellowed pages till I reached those leaves which Aunt Victoria had spoken about. I saw at once why they had caught her attention. For one thing they measured little more than 6 inches by 4 inches and the paper, besides being badly faded at the edges of the sheets, was ruled with faint lines. But even more striking was the difference in the handwriting. These pages were covered in a minute, cramped, cursive script quite unlike the hand of the Recording Clerk. If I had to select one adjective to describe it the word would be 'scholarly'. In fact the tiny writing put me immediately in mind of that of J. E. Lawless, my erstwhile tutor at St Catherine's; there were even some of the identical abbreviations – 'tho.' for 'though'; 'wd.' for 'would'; 'shd.' for 'should' – which I remembered he had favoured. Settling myself firmly into the corner closest to the window

I raised the book to catch the maximum amount of daylight and began to read.

Some twenty minutes before the train was due at Bristol I had reached the last entry. I find it quite impossible to describe accurately my precise state of mind at that moment. I remember becoming conscious of an acute headache the onset of which I had, presumably, ignored while I was engrossed in my reading. I remember too that as I unhooked my spectacles and gazed out of the window I experienced a most extraordinary sense of disorientation – perhaps 'displacement' would be the better word – as though the green fields and cosy Wiltshire farms beyond the track had become mysterious, insubstantial, illusory things; mere tokens of stasis in some fantastic temporal flux. The moment passed quickly enough – the discipline of a lifetime's ingrained habit of thought soon reasserted itself – but I was left with the same excessively unpleasant sense of inner quivering that I had once endured after experiencing a minor earthquake in Thessaloniki. To say that I doubted what I most firmly believed would be putting it too strongly: to say that my philosophical foundations had been temporarily shaken would not be putting it quite strongly enough.

It will, I am sure, be maintained that I am either the instigator of – or the victim of ! – some elaborate hoax. The first contention I shall perforce ignore, since, knowing it to be untrue, it does not particularly concern me. To the second I am forced to return a reluctant verdict of 'Not Proven'. I have had the Register examined by two separate experts in such matters and both have assured me, to my own total satisfaction, that the notebook pages which have been incorporated within it were stitched into the binding at the time when the book itself was bound up, i.e. not later than the middle of the eighteenth century and, in all likelihood, a good half century earlier. *Yet the paper of the notebook itself is, indisputably, of a type not manufactured before 1860! Ergo* either somebody is lying or the notebook is genuine.

If we assume that some person (unknown) had wished to perpetrate such a hoax, when could it have been done? From the internal evidence certainly not before 1894. Therefore this anonymous hoaxer must have had access to the Hertford Library, have inserted his spurious material into the register, have replaced it on the library shelf and then *done nothing at all to draw attention to it*. Since, presumably, the whole point of a hoax is to deceive as many people as possible this strikes me as just about the most pointless hoax ever devised.

That leaves, as far as I am concerned, only my Great Aunt Victoria. She had custody of the Register from the time of the sale in 1938 until the day of her death – ample opportunity certainly in which to have 'doctored it' to her heart's content. Furthermore she, with her professional connections, would have been ideally situated to carry out such a plan had she wished to do so. This would have entailed forging the whole 'diary' itself on suitable paper; having the Register broken down and the forged diary incorporated; re-assembling the whole and restoring it to its original condition in such a way as to totally deceive two vastly experienced and disinterested professional experts. She would also have had to insert (or have caused to be inserted) two completely spurious entries into the Register proper, doing it in such a way that there was no observable discrepancy between those false entries and the ones which preceded and followed them. The only way in which this could have been done would have been by removing two of the original sheets, obtaining two blank sheets of the identical seventeenth-century rag paper, forging the entries to correspond *exactly* with those in the rest of the book, and then re-assembling the whole. I am prepared to admit that all this *could* have been done, but nothing will ever succeed in convincing me that it was. Nevertheless, since such a thing is conceivably possible, I must to that extent accede to the verdict of 'Not Proven' on the second of my two counts.

Having said that, all that remains is for me to transcribe *in toto* the contents of this extraordinary document and to add, by way of an appendix, the relevant entries from the Register itself together with a few concluding observations of my own.

Although the transcript is a faithful word-for-word copy of the original text, I have taken the liberty of expanding the author's abbreviations, inserting the paragraphs, and tidying up the punctuation where I think it is called for. The diary commences at the top of the first page and it is possible that a preceding page or pages were lost before the others were in-corporated in the Register.

It is, of course, utterly pointless to go on cursing myself for my idiotic complacency, yet has there been a single waking hour in the last 48 when I have not done so? To assume, as I did, that the Morlocks* had done no more than carry out an investigation of the superficial structure of my Machine was an inexcusable indulgence in wishful thinking, bolstered, unfortunately, by my successful onward voyage and return. Yet even now I am by no means certain that the Morlocks were responsible for that microscopic fracture of the dexter polyhedron. Could it not equally well have occurred during that final frenzied battle within the pedestal of the White Sphinx? Indeed it seems more than likely. What is utterly unforgivable is that I should have failed to detect the flaw when I carried out my detailed check on the Machine on Friday. Well, few men can ever have paid more dearly for wanton carelessness.

I knew that something was amiss the moment I had recovered sufficiently from my initial vertigo to scan the dials. Instead of circling smoothly around the horologe the indicator arm had developed a perceptible and disquieting lurch, first slowing and then accelerating. I realized at once that two of the quartz pillars in the quincunx were out of phase and I suspected some minor fault of alignment which it would be but the work of a moment in the laboratory to correct. Although the dials on the fascia shewed that I was already well back into the seventeenth century, a glance at my pocket watch informed me that my journey was less than two minutes old. Very gingerly I coaxed the right-hand lever towards me and was much alarmed to observe that the pulsation of the needle at once became far more pronounced. This, together with that indescribable nausea which is seemingly an unavoidable concomitant of Time travel, produced in me a sensation that was uncomfortably close to panic. Nevertheless, I kept my head sufficiently to observe that I was not about to enter into conjunction with some massive external object and, very gently, I brought the lever back into the neutral position.

The machine was resting on the bare hillside, its brass runners buried in grass and buttercups. Above me the sun was blazing down out of a cloudless sky and from its position relative to the meridian I judged the hour to be early afternoon. Some way down the slope of the hill below me two brown and white cows were grazing placidly, flicking their tails at the flies. As I glanced away I saw one of them raise its head and regard me with mild curiosity. So much for the seventeenth century, I thought, and

* For this and similar references see *The Time Machine* by H. G. Wells. Ed.

with a silent prayer on my lips I thrust forward the left-hand lever which would send me winging forward through the centuries to 1894. *And nothing happened!* I tried again and even risked further pressure on the right-hand lever. The result was exactly the same.

My emotions at that moment were all but identical with those I had experienced when I first looked down from the gazebo on the hillcrest above the Hall of the Eloi and found my Machine was no longer standing where I had left it on the lawn before the White Sphinx. It is the fear that grips the marooned mariner when he sees the topsail finally dip below the horizon. For a minute or two I surrendered to it cravenly and then, thank Heaven! reason reasserted itself once more. I had successfully surmounted the earlier crisis: I should survive this too.

I climbed out of the saddle, stepped down into the grass, unclipped the aluminium cover and peered into the womb of the quincunx. One glance was sufficient to tell me what had happened. Of the four polyhedral quartz prisms, the second dexter one had *fractured clean into two along its plane of cleavage!*

For a long moment I simply stared at it in disbelief while the full implication of the disaster gradually dawned upon me. With it came an overwhelming awareness of the grotesque and inescapable irony of my predicament. There, a mere ten paces from where I was standing, lay my workbench, and lying upon that workbench were no fewer than *four identical quartz polyhedra* any one of which could have been fastened into place within a matter of moments! Ten paces or two hundred and thirty years! Compared with my previous voyage it was hardly a hairsbreadth of Time, and yet, for all that, those vital components might just as well have been engulfed in the swamps of the Jurassic.

I reached into the quincunx, unscrewed the two halves of the broken rod, withdrew them and examined them. I thought I could detect a minute scratch ending just where the fracture began. 'Ah, fool,' I castigated myself bitterly. 'Crass, unmitigated fool!'

I sat down in the grass with my back resting against the framework of the Machine, and tried to marshal my fragmented thoughts. It was plain enough that my only hope of escape was to obtain a replacement for that broken prism. I even derived a mite of consolation from the wry reflection that had it been the neodymium dodecahedron which had shattered I should have been lost indeed since that – chronically speaking – essential element had been discovered only in 1885! But how to set about obtaining a replacement?

I rose to my feet and consulted the fascia dials once more. A brief calculation told me that I was now in the year AD 1665. The date did indeed touch some faintly disturbing chord in my memory but I was too concerned with finding a solution to my immediate problem to spare any time on tracking it to its source. Reaching into the pannier below the saddle I next drew out the canvas knapsack and my Kodak. Then, mindful of my experience with the Morlocks, I unscrewed the two control levers thus still further immobilizing my already impotent Machine. That done I carefully removed the second of the dexter prisms, reasoning that, if a replacement were ever to be obtained, a complete artefact would provide a more satisfactory pattern than a broken one. These practical actions, small enough in themselves, did much to help me take that first imaginative step on the far side of the gulf which is imperative if a traveller in Time is to preserve the full effectiveness of his intellectual faculties.

My next move was to take stock of my useful possessions. I was, it is true, somewhat better equipped than when I had first launched myself so impulsively into the Future, but since I had planned for a brief expedition into the early Holocene it was open to question whether a patent pocket compass, a Kodak, a specimen case or a notebook and pencils would be of very much service to me in my present predicament. Far more to the point was the handful of loose change which, by a fortunate oversight, I was still carrying in one of the thigh pockets of my knicker-bockers. It amounted in all to two sovereigns, three florins, a six-pence and some assorted coppers. Apart from my fob watch, the other pockets surrendered little more than a small tin of liquorice cachous, my tobacco pouch and pipe, a box of lucifers, a twin-bladed pen-knife and a brass-sheathed pocket lens. This latter I put to immediate use by verifying what I had already suspected concerning the microscopic cause of the fracture in the prism.

The warmth of the summer sun was striking full upon me so I loosened the belt of my Norfolk jacket, hoisted the knapsack over my shoulder, and, after bidding my Machine a truly heart-felt *au revoir*, settled my cap square on my head and set off, striding out through the buttercups across the flank of the hill in the direction of Camberwell.

The plan of action I had settled upon was simple enough – to get to London as soon as I possibly could. It was there, if anywhere, that I might hope to find a skilled lapidary artificer whom I could prevail upon to fashion me a four-inch polyhedral rod of rock-crystal sufficiently accurate for my needs. An exact replica was obviously too much to hope for, but I reasoned that I had already sufficiently demonstrated how even a flawed rod would serve its purpose long enough to enable me to effect my return to the nineteenth century.

Ten minutes' brisk walking brought me within sight of the Thames basin, though the river itself I could perceive only as a tremulous silver flickering in the distance towards Rotherhithe some four miles to the north-east. I was astonished by the amount of woodland which clothed the south bank of the river from Battersea to Greenwich. Although it was largely dispersed in the form of small coppices and outgrown hedgerows, the spaces between those closest to me were filled by others yet more distant so that the general effect was to screen the City from my sight. Had I chosen to ascend to the crest of Herne Hill I would doubtless have obtained a view of the whole panorama, but time was too precious. Leaving the hilltop windmill on my left I descended by means of a dry and rutted cart-track towards the untidy huddle of houses which I guessed must be ancient Camberwell.

The track led me down into the road which I recognized as connecting Camberwell with Dulwich so I turned to my left and headed in the general direction of Walworth. As I rounded the corner which brought me in full view of the hamlet I was surprised to observe that a rough stockade had been erected across the road. The centrepiece of this makeshift barrier was formed by a large hay-wain, on the top of which were seated three men, one of whom appeared to be shouldering a musket. I paused for a moment to take stock of the situation then, able to make nothing of it, I approached to within hailing distance and called out to ask whether I was on the London road. 'Aye!' shouted one of the men, rising to his feet. 'And keep a-going, stranger! We're all sound bodies here and by the Lord's grace will stay so.'

Perplexed in the extreme I continued moving steadily towards them, whereupon the same man shouted again: 'Not one step further upon thy life!'

I halted in my tracks and stared at him – or rather at the musket which he was now pointing directly at my head! – and raised my hands to show that I carried no weapon. 'I wish you no harm, good people,' I cried.

'Nor we you, mister,' responded the spokesman. 'So get ye gone.'

'But this is most uncivil,' I protested. 'I have urgent business to transact in London.'

'Aye, and the Angel of Death likewise!' cried one of the others. 'Four thousand souls been culled at last week's billing.'

This extraordinary remark did what nothing else in the exchange had so far achieved. The significance of the final figure registered upon the dials of my Machine reverberated through my stunned mind like an electric alarum bell. *1665. The year of the Great Plague!*

My hands dropped to my sides as though paralysed and I stood transfixed, wonderstruck, staring at the three men. One of them raised his fingers to his lips and whistled shrilly. A moment later I caught the excited yelping of dogs. There was an urgent cry of 'Sic him! Sic him!', whereat I spun about and fled precipitately with a pack of eager curs snapping at my flying heels.

No sooner had I regained the sanctuary of the cart-track than the dogs, with a few backward looks and admonitory snarls, trotted off towards the village, leaving me with a painfully racing heart and the realization that my predicament was far worse than even I could have imagined. My historical knowledge of the effects of the Plague was woefully sketchy, though I did recollect from a childhood reading of Pepys' Diary that commercial life of some sort had continued in the City throughout the visitation. My longing to be quit for ever of this benighted age increased a hundredfold. I resolved to strike out at once across the fields in the general direction of Southwark, avoiding, as far as humanly possible, the vicinity of any of the scattered farms or hamlets I might encounter on the way.

An hour (and several wearisome detours) brought me within sight of the Old Kent Road along which I perceived a number of covered carts and several head of cattle being driven in the direction of London Bridge. I skirted round the edge of a cornfield, thrust my way through the hedge and, having gained the highway, set off at my best pace in the wake of this motley caravan. I soon came up with a young cattle drover who eyed me somewhat oddly, no doubt on account of my dress, though in truth my tweed knickerbockers were perfectly recognizable descendants of his own leather breeches and woollen hose. The most obvious anachronism was my chequered cloth cap (all the men I had seen so far had been wearing either the broad-brimmed 'wideawake' or the high-crowned 'steeple' style of headgear favoured by the Puritans) so on the pretence of wiping the sweat from my brow I removed the questionable article, stowed it away in my pocket, and gave the youth a good day. He returned my greeting civilly enough and enquired what I was travelling in. My look of perplexity led him to say: 'Are ye not a pedlar?'

It seemed prudent to agree that I was and I asked him whether he knew of any jewellers or instrument makers still trading in the City.

He shook his head and said he supposed they must all have fled if they had the means to do so. Realizing I should get no useful information from him and anxious to push on with all possible speed I wished him a good journey and strode off in the wake of the carts.

I was by now within plain sight of Southwark Cathedral and the Old Bridge and for the first time since setting foot in this grim century I found myself gazing about me with real curiosity. The great river – sparkling, green, and clear in a manner all but unimaginable in 1894 – was crowded with vessels of every conceivable shape and size from tiny skiffs to quite substantial merchantmen. Indeed, further down stream below the Tower I counted no fewer than twenty-three large craft moored out in mid-channel, while a host of small rowing boats fussed around them like water beetles. As to the City itself I think what struck me most forcibly was firstly the grisly row of severed heads adorning the battlements of the Bridge Gatehouse, and, secondly, the gaiety and brightness of the waterfront houses, each decorated individually to its owner's whim. The sight of those bright reflections shimmering on the sunny water affected me so strongly that it was with a real sense of impotence and loss that I suddenly realized how, within a mere twelvemonth, the ravages of the Great Fire would have destroyed for ever most of what I was now seeing. That it must be so I acknowledged, but it caused me none the less of a pang for that.

As I approached the Gatehouse I observed a group of watchmen armed with pikes and muskets examining the contents of the incoming carts and questioning the drivers. Since pedestrians did not appear to be attracting the same attention I strode on purposefully only to be halted by one of the guards demanding to know my business. I told him I was a pedlar-mechanician seeking out instrument makers in the City and added that I would be obliged if he could assist me with directions.

He looked me up and down, scrutinizing my woollen necktie and my stout Highland brogues with obvious suspicion. 'And whence come ye, master pedlar?' he asked.

'Canterbury,' I replied glibly, offering the first likely name that came to mind.

'Be ye of sound health?'

'Indeed I am,' I said, 'and hopeful to remain so.'

'Aye,' he muttered, 'with God's blessing, so are we all. Be advised by me, master, and look to peddle your wares elsewhere.'

'I have no choice in the matter,' I replied. 'My trade is too rare.' So saying I slid my hand into my trousers pocket and jingled my coins meaningfully. 'Would you happen to know of any jewellers still trading in the City?'

He squeezed his nose thoughtfully between his finger and thumb. 'Ludgate's their common quarter. But the sickness lies heavy thereabouts they say. More I know not.'

I thanked him for his help, drew out a penny from my pocket and handed it to him. As I hurried on to the bridge I glanced back and saw him turn the coin doubtfully between his fingers before tapping it against the steel blade of his pike.

I crossed the river without further incident, picked out the Gothic spire of Old St Paul's soaring high above the roofs to my left and knew that Ludgate lay immediately beyond it, hidden from my view. I passed through the gate at the north end of the bridge and stepped down into the City.

No sooner had I done so than the waterside breeze died away and I was assailed by a most terrible stench from the heaps of garbage and human ordure which lay scattered all down the centre of the street, baking in the sun and so thick with flies that the concerted buzzing sounded like a swarm of angry bees. I

127

felt my stomach heave involuntarily and clutched my handkerchief to my nose and mouth, marvelling how the other pedestrians seemed able to proceed about their business seemingly oblivious to the poisonous stench.

I had covered barely 200 yards before I came upon a house, securely shuttered and barred, with a clumsy cross daubed upon its door in red paint and the ominous words 'Lord, have mercy upon us', scrawled above it. Dozing on a stool beside it was an old man with a scarlet wooden staff resting across his knees. I observed that my fellow pedestrians were careful to give the area a wide berth and, at the risk of fouling my shoes, I too edged out towards the centre of the street, glancing up as I did so in time to see a small white face peeping fearfully down at me from behind one of the high leaded windows. In spite of the heat I shivered and quickened my pace, taking the first available turn to the left and hurrying down what is still, I believe, called Thames Street. As soon as I saw the cathedral spire rising to my right I turned again and headed towards it.

As I made my way along the narrow alley I scanned the signboards on either side and eventually saw one which bore a representation of a pair of compasses. I hurried towards it only to discover that the shop was locked and barred. I squinted in through the leaded window at the selection of terrestrial globes, astrolabes, hour-glasses and astronomical rings and felt my heart sink. What earthly hope had I of finding anyone capable of supplying my needs in an age which was only just beginning to emerge from the shadows of the medieval? As I turned dispiritedly away I saw an elderly gentleman emerging from a door further up the street. I waited until he came abreast of me and then accosted him politely and asked whether he knew of any instrument maker or optician still working in the neighbourhood.

Perhaps something in my manner of speech or my dress intrigued him because he peered at me shrewdly from beneath the broad brim of his hat and asked me if I would care to specify exactly what it was I was looking for.

Having nothing to gain by not doing so I told him I had urgent need of some skilled artificer capable of fashioning for me a small rod or cylinder of rock crystal.

'Why sir,' he said, 'if you seek a lens grinder then Master William Tavener is your man. His shop lies hard by St Anne's in Carter Lane.' He indicated with his cane the direction I should take, adding that he could not vouch for it that the man had not fled the City, though he believed not.

I thanked him warmly for his assistance and made haste to follow his directions. Ten minutes later I had found the shop, exactly where he had described it, with a large gilded spectacles frame hanging above it for its sign. I glanced briefly at the small display of reading lenses in the window, realized that this or nothing was what I had been seeking, and with a painfully racing heart reached for the door latch. To my inexpressible relief the door opened and I stepped over the threshold into the shop.

A small brass bell was standing on the wooden counter and, after waiting for a minute or so, I picked it up and rang it briskly. I heard a door bang somewhere in the back regions of the shop and the sound of approaching footsteps. Finally a young woman appeared holding a baby in her arms. She stood gazing at me sombrely for a moment then asked: 'What is it ye seek, master?'

'Is Mr Tavener in?' I asked. 'I have some urgent business for him.'

A distant voice called out: 'Who is it, Bessie?'

'Robert Pensley,' I supplied, '*Doctor* Robert Pensley.'

I thought I detected a faint quickening of interest in her face as she passed on this information. 'He'll be down to you in a minute, sir,' she said.

'Does he work alone then?'

'Th' prentices have flown this month past,' she said. 'I warrant I'd have followed them had it not been for father. Plague or no plague he'll not budge.'

'Have you any rats in your house?' I inquired.

'Aye, some I dare say. What house hereabouts hasn't? They swarm up from the Fleet like black heathens.'

'Their fleas are the plague carriers,' I said. 'Rid yourself of the rats and you'll be safe.'

She laughed. 'Lord sir, the beasts are dying without any help from us! I found two lying stiff in the jakes this very morning.'

'You didn't touch them?'

'Not I,' she said. 'Father hoisted them with the furnace tongs and flung 'em over the wall into the ditch.'

'On no account handle them whatever you do,' I said. 'One bite from an infected flea and that could well be the death of you. Believe me, I know.'

'They do say as it's the foul air,' she said. 'There's orders posted abroad for the Watch to burn night fires at every street crossing – and all day long in the open yards. But Father says the London air's always been as foul even when there was no plague.'

'He's right,' I insisted. 'So do as I say, Bessie, and promise me you'll touch no dead rats, then you and your babe will both live through it safely.'

She smiled. 'Me, I hate the ugly brutes. Hark ye, here comes Father now.'

A middle-aged man with a bald crown to his head and sparse brown hair touched with grey, came shuffling out of the passage at the back of the counter and nodded to me. 'We've not met before, I think sir,' he said. 'What is it ye seek?'

I lifted my knapsack on to the counter, unbuckled it and drew out the complete prism and the two broken pieces. 'I want you to cut me an eight-faced crystal prism to these identical dimensions, Mr Tavener,' I said. 'Can you do it?'

He took the whole crystal from me and held it up, twisting it this way and that as he squinted at it. 'May I ask who fashioned this for ye, sir?'

'I had it cut in Italy.'

''Tis fine workmanship. I've seen none better.' And with that he handed it back to me with a smile.

'But you must keep it, Mr Tavener,' I insisted. 'It is to be your pattern. The dimensions are vital, I do assure you.'

'I'm sorry to disappoint ye, Doctor,' he said, 'but seemingly that's what I must do. Single-handed I'm so tardy in my work that it would be the best part of a three-month before I could even consider it. Why, I have grinding in hand upstairs for Master Hooke, due last month, that bids fair to keep me till the middle of next.'

'Mr Tavener,' I cried desperately, 'I have not travelled all this way to find you, only to be denied! Will you tell me how long it would take to cut such a prism?'

He lifted the rod again and turned it over speculatively between his fingers. 'Cut *and* polish?' he inquired.

'Of course.'

'Two or three days, maybe. Depending on how fine ye wanted it.'

'And what would you charge?'

'A guinea a day for the skilled labour.'

'I'll pay you ten,' I said, and the words were no sooner out of my mouth than I realized what I had said.

He peered up at me quizzically over the crystal. 'Ten guineas?' he repeated slowly. 'Ye'd pay me *ten gold guinea pieces*?'

I nodded. 'I will. Providing you'll put the work in hand for me at once.'

He looked down again at the prism and traced its bevelled contours with his fingertips. I could see he was wondering what kind of a man I was to have brought him such a proposition. 'D'ye mind telling me why the matter is so urgent, sir?'

'You'd not believe me if I did, Mr Tavener,' I said, 'but I assure you it could well be a matter of life or death. Time is of the essence.'

'Well, there again, sir,' he said, 'I know not whether I even have such a blank to suit. Like all else good crystal's hard to come by in these black days. But perhaps you'd care to step up into the workshop and see what there is.'

'Then you *will* undertake it?'

'If I have no satisfactory blank, sir, then no amount of willing on my part will make ye one,' he said. 'So you'd best come up and see for yourself.'

I followed him through the shop, up some dark stairs and into a long, low-beamed workroom which must surely have been cantilevered on to the back of the house. Windows ran round three sides and two of them looked out over the graveyard of the church next door. The early evening sunlight was slanting in through a dusty drapery of cobwebs. An antique wooden treadle lathe stood against one wall. Suspended above it was a rack of tools. Instead of a fireplace there was a charcoal oven-furnace and a glass-making crucible. The whole place was depressingly reminiscent of a Dürer engraving of an alchemist's glory-hole, but while Mr. Tavener was routing in the depths of a cupboard I examined two lenses I found lying on a bench and discovered them to be of astonishingly high quality.

Tavener emerged clasping a chunk of quartz which he brought across to the bench and laid before me. 'That's Tintagel pebble,' he said. 'Would it do?'

I picked up the crystal and held it to the light. As far as I could tell it was flawless. I handed it back to him and expelled my breath in a long sigh. 'It will do perfectly, Mr Tavener,' I said.

At that very moment the clock in the church began to sound a chime and, without thinking, I pulled my watch from my fob pocket, intending to set it by the prevailing time. I had just clicked open the gold face-guard when I noticed that Tavener's gaze was riveted on the instrument. I smiled. 'You will not have seen a watch like this, I dare say, Mr Tavener?' I detached the chain clip and held the instrument out to him.

He took it from me and turned it round wonderingly in his fingers, rather as the guard at the Bridge Gatehouse had turned over the penny I had given him. Then he lifted it to his ear and a look of the most profound astonishment suffused his face. It is, in truth, a fine timepiece, made by Jacques Simenon of Paris and given to me to mark my twenty-first anniversary by my dear mother and father. I took it back from him, opened the case with my thumbnail and showed him the jewelled precision movement within. 'Why sir,' he breathed, 'that is a true miracle! God's truth, never in my life did I dream to see such a thing.'

'I warrant it is the only one of its kind in the world today,' I said.

'That I can well believe, sir. I doubt the King himself hath such a treasure.'

'Mr Tavener,' I said slowly, 'would *you* like to own that watch?'

He looked at me as if I had gone clean out of my mind and said nothing at all.

'I mean it,' I said. 'So anxious am I to have the prism cut that I am prepared to give you my watch in exchange for it. It is worth far more than ten guineas. Make for me a perfect copy of that prism, put it into my hand, and I will put the watch into yours. See, here is my hand in pledge of it.'

Tavener looked down at the watch ticking away merrily on the bench with the yellow sunlight winking from the jewelled balance. It almost seemed to have hypnotized him 'Well?' I said. 'Isn't it a fair bargain?'

'Aye sir,' he agreed at last. 'I must suppose ye best know what ye are about,' and with that he joined his palm to mine and we shook upon the contract.

'And when can you start?' I asked him.

'Tomorrow, God willing. But I shall have to ride to Edmonton first for pumice powder and rottenstone. I'm clean out of both of them.'

'How long will that take?'

'All day, most like. 'Tis ten mile there and no less back.'

'And those things you must have?'

'Aye. For cutting pebble. 'Tis not like your whoreson glass. The other grits I have enough of.'

'It's not for me to teach you your business, Mr Tavener,' I said. 'All I can do now is wish you God speed.'

'Believe me, I'll not tarry sir. As it is the lass won't care to be left.'

I picked up the watch and clipped it back on to its chain. 'I am just newly arrived in London, Mr Tavener,' I said, 'and as yet have no lodgings. Could you perhaps recommend me to some inn close by?'

He scratched his chin. 'The Three Keys in Lower Wharf Street is a clean house,' he said. 'It's just down alongside Paul's Steps. I dare say that would suit ye. The air is more wholesome by the water.'

So I took my leave of him with my heart feeling a good deal lighter than it had for many hours. I soon found The Three Keys and prevailed upon the landlord to rent me an attic room overlooking the river, paying for one week's rent and board in advance with the first of my two sovereigns. I told him that the coin was a Polish *thaler* – Henderson the numismatist once told me that this coin bore a superficial resemblance to our modern sovereign – and he accepted it cheerfully enough, no doubt on account of his having frequent dealings with sailors from foreign ports. I drank a mug of ale with him and ate an excellent mutton pasty while he regaled me with horrific stories of the ravages the 'visitation' was wreaking upon the City. He also told me that the ships I had seen drawn up in mid-stream were filled with wealthy citizens who had embarked their wives and families and would permit no one else to set foot aboard, all their daily needs being supplied by boatmen who purchased food on shore, rowed out with it, and loaded it into baskets which were then hauled up on deck.

Soon after this I retired to my room intending to take a short nap, but whether from the unaccustomed effect of the strong ale or by simple reaction to the day's exertions, I fell deeply asleep and did not wake until the next morning, though I seem dimly to recall having my dreams invaded by the sound of a handbell being rung in the street below and the jarring clatter of iron-shod cart wheels upon cobble stones.

Apart from a brief excursion this morning along the water-front, during which I purchased for myself a less anachronistic hat with one of my three florins and a plain-fronted, linen bib shirt with another, I have spent the whole day closeted in my attic writing up this record of what must surely be one of the most extraordinary days ever spent by a nineteenth-century gentleman.

August 28th. To Tavener's early, only to find the shop locked up. I waited for over half an hour hoping that at least his daughter would put in an appearance but saw nobody. I made my way round to the back of the premises and peered up at the workshop windows. The whole place seemed utterly deserted. The rest of the morning I spent wandering about the City in an agony of apprehension. Finally I returned to Carter Street, knocked on the door of the house adjoining the shop and inquired whether they knew anything of the man's whereabouts. The woman told me that Tavener, accompanied by his daughter and her child, had set out early the previous morning in a small pony cart and had not been seen since. Telling myself they had been delayed at Edmonton and would surely return that afternoon, I wandered into the Cathedral and, despite my own anxiety, was deeply moved by the sight of hundreds of people all kneeling in silent prayer. I read a printed proclamation which I found nailed up in the Cathedral porch. It was signed by the Lord Mayor and the Sheriffs and gave a series of orders to the citizens, some of which explained the odd noises I had heard – handbells, horns blowing and the rest. Nothing more desperately ironical than the directions *to kill all dogs and cats*! – the one slender hope of keeping some of the rats out of the houses! Returned to Tavener's three times more, then finally back here feeling thoroughly depressed.

August 29th. Spent a wretched night lying awake listening to the melancholy cries of the bellmen – '*Bring out your de-a-a-d! Bring out your de-a-a-d!*' Resolved to try to speak to the Mayor or the Sheriffs and attempt to persuade them to at least rescind the order for the destruction of dogs and cats. Heard the squeaking of mice – or rats! – behind the wainscot and broke out into a cold sweat of pure terror. Would I not be better advised to seek lodgings south of the river?

(Later) Still no sign or word of Tavener. Wrote him a note which I thrust under his door, urging him to contact me immediately he returns. Found another lens grinder in Cheapside but lacking the prisms which I had left with Tavener I could only give him a rough description of what I wanted. Since he had no suitable crystal anyway it was so much wasted effort. However he told me that William Tavener was 'a true man of his word' and that my business could not be in better hands. Consolation of a sort, I suppose, if only I could be sure that my business *was* in his hands!

A thoroughly unnerving encounter in a street (Bread St?) linking Cheapside with Watling Street. Saw a man I took for a drunkard staggering towards me. Just before he reached me he pitched over and fell full length on the cobbles. I hurried up to him – he was lying on his face – turned him over and saw to my horror that he had all the signs of the Plague, gross swellings at the sides of his neck and dark blotches under his skin from internal bleeding. There was a trickle of blood running from the corner of his mouth though this may well have been a result of his fall. He was still breathing – a throaty, rasping sound – and as I bent over him he vomited up a black, evil-smelling bile, shuddered once, violently, and lay still. I looked up and saw that the narrow street which had been busy enough when I entered it was now completely deserted. All round me I heard the staccato sounds of doors and window shutters being clapped to. I felt for the poor devil's pulse and found nothing. I left him lying there in the street and hurried away.

When I had recovered something of my composure I made my way straight to the Mansion House and asked if I could speak to one of the Sheriffs or some other person of authority upon a matter of great urgency. Finally I was granted an audience with a Mr Robinson, the Private Secretary to Sir Charles Doe. He listened patiently while I poured out my reasons for at least rescinding the order for the destruction of cats and dogs. Having heard me out he thanked me politely and then told me that I was mistaken since it had been proved quite conclusively that the plague was transmitted by the 'evil miasma' which was inhaled by these very animals and then breathed out upon their unspecting victims! Besides, he added with a charming smile, did I really suppose that such a tiny creature as a *flea* could carry all the monstrous weight of such appalling infection? Furthermore, if extra proof were needed, could any man deny that fleas had been skipping around London for years before the outbreak of the present calamity? 'Bubonic plague,' I said, 'is carried by the black rat in the form of an invisible bacterium, *bacillus pestis*. When the rats die of the infection their fleas seek out other hosts and by sucking their blood transmit the infection to them. Would you be so good as to record that fact and see that it is conveyed to Sir John Lawrence? If the authorities act promptly thousands of innocent lives may yet be saved.' Mr Robinson smiled and nodded and scribbled something on a piece of paper. 'I will see that your message is conveyed to His Lordship, Doctor Pensley,' he said. 'And now I really must beg ye to excuse me for I have a great deal of most pressing business to attend to.' And that was that.

August 30th. It is now three whole days since I spoke to Tavener and still nothing. Last night, for the first time, I found myself the victim of a most dreadful depression which I could not shake off. All day long a heavy pall of cloud has hung over the City and my eyes are still red and inflamed from the sulphurous smoke of those infernal bonfires they light *to sweeten the air*! This afternoon I was assailed by an ungovernable panic fear that my Machine had been discovered and removed. I ran down to the waterside, paid a boatman sixpence to ferry me over to Southwark and made my way back across the fields to Herne Hill. My relief at discovering my Machine was still standing exactly where I had left it – and, apparently, untouched – quite overwhelmed me. I sank down in the grass beside it and wept like a child. While I was making my return a violent thunderstorm broke and by the time I eventually got back to the inn I was soaked to the skin. The landlord persuaded me to drink a stiff tot of hot Hollands punch which, though it may not be the universal specific he claims, certainly seems to have done something to lift my leaden spirits.

August 31st. Tavener is returned!! The serving maid who attends on me in my room brought up my clothes which had been drying overnight in the kitchen and told me that Tavener's daughter had brought word to the inn-keeper. My spirits soared like a skylark. I was out of bed, had dressed, and was on my way to Carter Street within minutes of hearing the news. Bessie came to the shop door herself and told me that her father was already at work upstairs on my commission. Not wishing to delay him still further I asked her to tell me what had happened. Whereupon she invited me through into their parlour and told me how they had been stopped at Stanford by a barrier across the road, similar in all respects to that which I had encountered at Camberwell. Unable to persuade the villagers to let them through they had been forced to make a detour as far westward as Palmer's Green before they could circle back by a maze of by-lanes towards Edmonton. They had spent that night under a haystack and, on resuming their journey next morning, had reached Edmonton around noon only to find to their dismay that there a similar barricade had been erected. Her father had spent most of that afternoon parleying with the constables and had eventually prevailed upon them to allow him through. But their troubles were still not over. The dealer who normally supplied him with materials had shut up his works for the duration of 'the visitation' and gone to lodge with his sister in Newmarket! Having got so far the resourceful Tavener was not to be denied. He forced an entry into the store shed, helped himself to whatever he wanted, left some money to pay for it together with a note of explanation and, next morning, the three of them were on their way back to London.

All had gone well until, while they were descending Stanford Hill, the axle of their hired pony-cart broke. Tavener was somehow able to effect a temporary repair which enabled them to crawl back to Wood Green where they had spent the rest of that day finding a wheelwright and persuading him to replace the broken axle. This meant still further delay and by the time the job was finished it was too late to continue to London. They spent that night in Wood Green and had set out the following day, arriving back at Carter Lane at about the same time as I was on my way back from Herne Hill.

I have recounted here briefly what Bessie Tavener spent an animated hour in describing, painting a remarkably vivid word picture of the pathetic bands of fugitives from the City whom they had encountered roaming the forest round Woodford – 'living like gipsies, poor souls, with nary a scantling of provender to keep their bones from rattling.' I was moved to ask her

137

whether she regretted having to return to London but she said there were already many cases of plague in the outlying districts and if she was fated to die of it she would rather draw her last breath in her own house than lost among strangers. I repeated my stern warning about the rats and extracted a solemn promise from her that she would keep well clear of any place where fleas might be caught. She gave me her word readily enough, but I suspect it was more to humour me than because she believed me.

I looked in briefly upon Tavener before I left and told him how inexpressibly relieved I was to see him back. He merely nodded, gave me a shy grin, and returned to his lathe. As I stepped out into the street, which smelt mercifully sweeter for the deluge yesterday evening, I felt as though a huge and suffocating burden had been lifted from my shoulders.

September 1st. The soaking I received in the thunderstorm seems to have left me with a chill. Hardly surprising. However, I have before me one of the landlord's excellent 'Hollands tonics' which is a great source of comfort. Shortly before noon I called round at Tavener's to see how the work was progressing only to find him engaged in packing up a box of lenses for a little hunch-backed fellow in a grubby wig. Tavener introduced him to me as 'Master Hooke'. As I shook him by the hand I thought, by way of a joke, to say: '*ut tensio sic vis*, Mr Hooke.' He gave me a most extraordinary look as if to say: 'Who is this madman I have by the hand?' and the thought crossed my mind that perhaps he had not yet formulated that shortest of all Physical Laws which posterity would link to his name. Thereafter we chatted in a desultory way about the Plague until he hobbled off with his box of lenses under his arm.

After he had gone Tavener showed me how the work on the prism was progressing. The blank is already two-thirds shaped in rough and he hopes to have that part of the work completed by this evening. Then the labour of polishing begins. In spite of my pressing him he would not give me a definite date for completion on the grounds that Tintagel pebble was notoriously slow to take a fine polish being 'hard nigh unto diamond'. He is certainly a most meticulous craftsman who obviously takes a profound – though somewhat inarticulate – pride in the quality of his work.

September 2nd. A violent bout of sweating in the night left me with a feeling of great lassitude and a severe headache. I arose late, dressed myself, went out into the street and was overcome with a fit of giddiness not unlike the vertigo I have experienced while Time travelling. I have no doubt at all that it is an unwelcome after-effect of the chill, but I could well do without it. On my returning to the inn the landlord made my blood run cold with a story of some poor pregnant girl in Cripplegate who was nailed up in her house when one of her sisters contracted the Plague. All the rest of the family were stricken down one after the other until finally, when only she was left alive, she gave birth and, with no one on hand to help her, died, not of the Plague, but of a haemorrhage! With her self-delivered infant in her arms! The sheer, wanton cruelty of this policy of sealing up houses is almost beyond belief. No phrase sickens me more than the pious: ''Tis God's will', and I must be hearing it in one form or another twenty times a day.

September 3rd. Little doubt in my mind but that I've caught a really nasty dose of influenza. I have passed all the day lying in bed and, despite the sun beating down on the tiles overhead making this attic as hot as an oven, I have spent much of the time shivering violently. When the servant girl came up to make my bed I told her I had caught a bad chill and asked her to be good enough to fetch me up a mug of strong spiced ale. That was over three hours ago and still she has not returned.

September 9th? Hostel of St Barnabas. Days of nightmare. What is memory? What dream? Grey Morlock figures bending over me, prodding at my chest, thrusting me into my clothes, carrying me downstairs with a rag soaked in brandy stuffed into my mouth. A boat. Stars swirling round in the sky above me. Squeaking of oars. Voices whispering. Waking again to find the sun hammering nails into my naked eyes. My knapsack is lying on the sand beside me. Where am I? My fumbling fingers explore my body as though it is a stranger's. My joints are all on fire and my head feels as though a red-hot gimlet is being screwed into my brain. Beneath my armpit the outline of an unfamiliar lump. Another in my groin. *Buboes!* Pain gives way to sheer, mindless terror. I am falling backwards down the black well-shaft that has no bottom. Voices. Hands lifting me. Hands carrying me. Falling, falling without end. I open my eyes to see a stone vaulted roof arching above me. As I stare up at it a cowled face swims into my field of vision. Its lips move. 'Welcome, stranger.' 'Where am I?' (is that really my own voice?) 'The hostel of Saint Barnabas.' 'I have the Plague?' The cowl nods. 'Am I dying?' 'We think not.' Time passes. I sleep; I dream; I wake. Sleep: dream: wake. Strong, firm, gentle hands raise me and prop me back against straw-filled sacks. Soup is spooned into my mouth and a worried voice urges: 'Drink, Robert.' I swallow and choke. 'Again.' I swallow. 'Again. Good i'faith. Most excellently done.' 'Who brought me here?' 'Who knows, Robert? Friends to be sure. They could have drowned ye in the river like a puppy for all ye could have stayed them.' A pause, then: 'Who is Weena?' 'Weena?' 'Aye. Ye called on her by the hour in your raving. Dost wish me to send word to her that ye lie here?' 'She's dead.' He rises from my bedside and sketches a token blessing over me. 'My knapsack,' I croak. 'Fear not, Robert. 'Tis here.' He lifts it on to my bed and then moves off down the ward. I fumble the buckle undone, extract my note-book and force myself to write a note to Tavener. Then I sleep again. When I wake next I make this entry. It has taken me nearly three hours to complete it.

September 11th. Today Brother James trimmed my beard for me and has promised to see that my note is delivered to Tavener. He assures me too that 'through God's infinite mercy' I have successfully weathered the worst of the storm. Twenty four patients have died since I was brought in. The bell in the chapel never seems to stop its mournful tolling.

September 12th. The superstitious fear of infection is presumably what I have to thank for the fact that I still have all my possessions down to the last pencil – that and the fact that the innkeeper's livelihood was at stake. Had word got out that I had the Plague The Three Keys would now be a 'sealed house'.

September 13th. This afternoon I spent half an hour trying to persuade Brother Dominic, the physician, that the infection is transmitted primarily by rats and their fleas. I had hardly more success than I had with Secretary Robinson even though I thought to cite Harvey to illustrate how the bacillus was carried through the bloodstream. B.D. told me he thought it was an interesting theory but that proof was lacking. I told him that if he swabbed out his wards with a 250/1 solution of sulphuric acid he'd soon have all the proof he needed. 'And what is sulphuric acid, Robert?' On my telling him it was another name for oil of vitriol he nodded, but I suspect he was really no more convinced than Robinson had been.

September 14th. A message was brought in to me by a walking patient that a Master William Tavener was without and would speak with me but was fearful of entry. He sent word to say that the work was finished and that he had it now upon him. On hearing this I crawled off my bed, staggered the length of the ward like a drunkard and so, by painful degrees, proceeded to the Hostel gate. 'Tavener?' I croaked. 'Is that you, man?' He stood a little way off and stared in at me. 'In God's name, Doctor Pensley, ye are sadly changed!' 'I'm recovered now,' I said, clutching at the iron rails of the gate for support. 'It's quite safe to come close.' 'That I durst not, Doctor,' he called. 'Go ye back a way and I'll push them through to ye.' I did as he said, though how I contrived to remain standing is a miracle, where-upon he ran to the gate and quickly thrust a bundle wrapped in cloth through on to the flagstones. I picked it up, unwrapped it with shaking hands and found, lying inside, swaddled in lambs-wool, the two whole prisms together with the two broken pieces. *And for the life of me I could not tell the copy from the original!* My eyes filled with tears I was quite powerless to prevent. 'God bless you, William Tavener!' I cried. 'You are indeed a master among craftsmen!' and taking out my watch and chain I held them up so that he could see them plainly, then laid them down upon the flagstones. He let the watch lie there while I stepped back, then he darted forward and scooped it into a leather bag he had ready for the purpose. 'Farewell, Doctor,' he called. 'God be wi'ye!' and he was gone. Somehow I managed to stagger back to the ward and there collapsed upon my cot.

September 15th. Feel too weak to write much. Obviously overdid things yesterday. The prism is a true marvel – a perfect replica. No doubt at all it will fulfil its function.

September 16th. Vomiting all last night. Feel v. weak.

September 17th. Diarrhoea and vomiting.
disgust

There it ends. The last entry is so faintly pencilled that it is very difficult to decipher. The word could possibly be read as 'despair'. However, the Register itself leaves us in no doubt as

141

to the final outcome. One of the two entries for 20th September, 1665 reads: *'Decd. at ye 5th hr, one Rbt. Penly* (sic) *of med. yrs. of ye black flux.'* It is matched by a previous entry for 5th September: *'Admi. one Penly, sick nigh unto death.'*

In the weeks which followed my initial perusal of the Hertford Manuscript I took certain steps to ascertain, for my own satisfaction, whether the journal was in fact nothing more than an elaborate and pointless forgery.

My first problem was to obtain a specimen of the true Doctor Pensley's handwriting. I wrote to Somerset House and inquired whether he had left a Will, only to be informed that there was no one of that name in their probate records for the years 1894–1899. I then thought to try the civil records for Herne Hill and wrote to the Camberwell Town Clerk, but again drew a blank. I could find no 'Pensley' in the London Telephone Directory, and a discreet advertisement placed in the Personal Column of *The Times* proved just as unrewarding. However, these initial disappointments served only to spur my determination. I contacted an old friend of mine in Cambridge and asked him to consult the University Records on my behalf. Within a fortnight I learnt that Robert James Pensley had been admitted to Emmanuel College as an Exhibitioner in the year 1868.

I travelled down to Cambridge and there in the College Records I found at last what I had been seeking. It was not very much certainly – a mere signature – but when I laid it beside an entry in the Hertford text where the author had written out his own name, I was convinced that the writing was by the same hand. My instinctive conviction has since been confirmed by the opinion of a professional graphologist.

My next move was to consult the back files of local newspapers. The only one which still survives is The *Dulwich and District Observer* and there, in the yellowed print of the issue for the week of 18th June 1894, tucked away among advertisements for safety bicycles and patent knife powder, I found: *Puzzling Disappearance of Well-Known Amateur Scientist.* The account, written in an excruciatingly 'literary' style, described how Doctor Robert Pensley, the only surviving son of James and Martha Pensley, had vanished from his home in Herne Hill on the morning of June 7th and had not been seen or heard from since. There was a thinly veiled suggestion that the doctor had been suffering from severe mental strain brought on by overwork. His housekeeper, in an exclusive interview with 'our Reporter', described how her employer was in the habit of vanishing into his laboratory 'for hours on end, bless him, and all night too sometimes'. There the article ended and since I could find no further references to the mystery in any later issue, I can only suppose that the matter had been purposely hushed up.

But I could not let the matter rest there. Some strange, haunting quality in that pencilled manuscript beckoned to me like a forlorn will-o'-the-wisp, and I resolved to track down as many of the historical references as it was possible to do after an interval of over three hundred years. During the past eighteen months, whenever I have had the opportunity, I have consulted ancient documents in the Guildhall, the Stationers' Hall, the British Museum and the London Records Office in an attempt to verify what I already *felt* to be true, namely that, in some wholly inexplicable manner, Robert Pensley *had* succeeded in transferring himself backwards in time to the seventeenth century and had there perished.

My first notable success was in establishing that one William Tavener, a member of the Guild of Spectacle Makers, had occupied premises next to the Church of St Anne in Carter Lane. The date given was 1652. A further entry recorded that two apprentices had been found to the aforesaid Master Tavener at premises in New Cheapside in 1668! So he, at least, seems to have escaped both the Plague and the Fire.

In a Victorian handbook entitled *The Inns of Elizabethan London* I came upon a reference to The Three Keys of Lower Wharf Street. Like most of the other establishments mentioned it was destroyed in the Great Fire of 1666.

The Hostel of Saint Barnabas – a Franciscan Charity Foundation – is reasonably well documented. It functioned until the early nineteenth century when it was pulled down to make way for a new dockyard.

Last May, in the archives of the Mansion House, I unearthed the name of one Samuel Robinson Esq., recorded as having been appointed to the post of *amanuensis privatus* to Sir Charles Doe, Sheriff, in the year 1663.

In 1665 Robert Hooke was certainly in London, working as 'curator of Experiments' for the newly founded Royal Society, and I have no reason to doubt that he would have called upon the services of Master Tavener to supply him with his optical apparatus. Incidentally, it might not be inappropriate to point out that Robert Hooke, as well as formulating his famous Law, has also been credited with a multitude of other discoveries, among them the invention of the spring balance wheel without which the science of horology (not to mention navigation) would doubtless have languished for many years longer in the Dark Ages!

Yet, when all is said and done, such 'facts' as I have been able to disinter seem to raise more questions than they answer. I feel I am for ever condemned to pace the circumference of a circle which turns out to be not a circle at all but a spiral – my point of arrival is never the same as my point of departure. For to accept the Hertford Manuscript at its face value must surely mean accepting a concept in which Time is both predetermined and yet infinite, an endless snake with its tail in its own mouth, a cosmos in which the Past and the Future coexist and will continue to do so for all Eternity.

How then is it that I both *can* and *do* believe that Robert Pensley's journal, written in his own hand in the year 1665, was already lying there gathering dust on a shelf in the library of Hertford Castle for fifty years before its author had drawn his first infant breath in the year 1850? Or that he died, most horribly, on a straw pallet in a charity hospital in the district of Wapping, beside the silver Thames, clutching in his stiffening fingers a fragment of polished rock crystal which he had staked his life to obtain, only to lose the wager at the very moment when he must surely have believed that he had won?